She cut him off. "Justin, let me do my job and you do yours, okay?"

"You're clear," Justin instructed, "Crank it up."

Although she could no longer see him, she heard him. She was more frightened than she had ever been in her life, and knowing he was there gave her a sense of calm.

Cass flipped the ignition switch and the engine roared to life. She looked down and checked her gauges: water temperature, oil pressure, and tachometer.

Everything was good.

She eased down the clutch and slipped the car into first gear, her excitement mounting and rising with each movement. Pressing the accelerator, she mapped her path and released the clutch and brake. Then she slammed down on the accelerator and she was off.

The power, the pull and the exhilaration of the car under her sent her whooping for joy, and the race, for her, was on. Second gear onto the straight away, third gear going into the turn, the g-forces on the car pulling her toward the wall, then those same forces yanking her body toward the passenger side of the car as she grabbed fourth and exited turn two.

Both gloved hands gripped the trembling wheel. The power of the car shook the whole frame and it was a heady feeling.

I was born to do this.

She rounded the fourth curve heading for the front stretch. This was what she had dreamed of. She needed to get a feel for the car and the track. The best way to do that was to run at full throttle, otherwise she wouldn't get a real sense for what she was up against. She suddenly wanted to beat the odds—the first woman to make it in the series. She could almost taste it.

What Reviewers are saying about Racing Hearts…

…Although Racing Hearts is a sensual treat, the developing relationship between Just and Cass takes a starring role. This hot hero and spunky heroine have an undeniable chemistry that hooks the reader early on and doesn't let go until the last word.
*4 Stars, Susan Mitchell
Romantic Times BookClub*

"Hot, sensual and wildly romantic … definitely an author to add to your auto-buy list!"
*5 unicorns, Recommended Read
Enchanted in Romance*

"…masterfully captured the suspense and excitement of motor sport. …a gripping story, with depth, which combines a fabulous romance with detailed insight into the electrifying and often breathtaking world of NASCAR."
*5 Angels, Recommended Read, Jane
Fallen Angel Reviews*

"…ability to draw the reader into the world of her creation is fantastic … will take you on a 200mph ride … and never let you go."
*5 angels, Mary
Fallen Angels Reviews*

"…sensual and heart-pounding … great book that has sex, drama, and unexpected … situations."
*5 Cups, Sheryl
Coffee Time Romance*

Racing Hearts

By

Rae Monet

Liquid Silver Books
Indianapolis, Indiana

This is a work of fiction. The characters, incidents, and dialogues in this book are products of the author's imagination and are not to be construed as real. Any resemblance to actual events or persons, living or dead, is entirely coincidental..

Copyright © 2004 Rae Monet

All rights reserved. No part of this publication may be reproduced, stored in a retrieval system, or transmitted in any form or by any means, electronic, mechanical, recording or otherwise, without the prior written permission of the publisher

Published By:
Liquid Silver Books
10509 Sedgegrass Dr.
Indianapolis, IN 46235

Liquid Silver Books publishes books online and in trade paperback. Visit our site at http://www.liquidsilverbooks.com

Manufactured in the United States of America

ISBN: 1-59578-109-9

Cover: April Martinez

Prologue

"This is the one I want," Margaret Kingsdale commanded as she carelessly tossed a blue multi-part folder in front of her son, Albert.

The folder snapped open, displaying a photo of a naturally beautiful, fresh-faced young woman. Long golden strands of hair blew across a glowing face, lit up with a glorious smile. Bright blue eyes, high, sculpted cheekbones and small straight nose seemed as if they belonged on the face of royalty instead of a racecar driver.

Albert gulped.

She has that girl-next-door, sweet, sexy look—so incredible.

Albert sighed at his mother's choice. Of the six women the private detective had presented, this one's profile was the most interesting.

"Cassandra Jamison is said to be reckless, Mother. Not easy to control."

He lifted the folder and studied the woman closer. Cassandra was leaning against a black motorcycle, outfitted in form-fitting black leather, a full-faced black helmet resting in her small, feminine hands.

There was something about the woman that aroused him. Maybe it was a feeling that she was wild, perhaps even uncontrollable. Along with the mischief in her eyes, he saw a challenge.

Taming Cassandra, he decided, would be worth the effort.

"She lost her parents in a car wreck when she was young and raised her baby sister. She sort of gave up her racing career after that."

Margaret extracted a cigarette from her jewel-studded 24-carat gold case. She lit the cigarette drawing on it like she was sucking all the life out of it.

"Cassandra Jamison's beauty and spirit will fit our plan perfectly," she drawled.

Their plan, Albert thought, cringing. So unbelievable and crazy, it might work. Lovely Cosmetics was the largest grossing, leading producer in the cosmetics industry. However, as of late, they had been losing market share to their arch competitor, Narella Cosmetics, innovative advertising campaign, Women at Work.

Women all over the world were connecting with the idea that they could do anything and still remain feminine. It had earned Narella three percent of the cosmetics market share in two months and it was still climbing. Even three percent was a devastating blow to Lovely Cosmetics.

Margaret Kingsdale, Albert reflected, was one of the most shrewd, influential female business figures of the century, and when she made a decision it usually made them money.

Lovely Cosmetics' plan was to sponsor the first female stock car driver to break into the male-dominated Nextel Cup Racing Series.

The campaign was targeted at the over forty percent female fans of the NASCAR circuit. His mother calculated they would gain back their lost market share and more.

"Are you sure?" Albert said.

"How old is she?"

"She just turned twenty-one."

"Is she well respected in the field?" Mrs. Kingsdale took another pull on her cigarette.

"Very."

"Does she have a husband? Boyfriend?" Finishing her first cigarette, his mother crushed it out and reached for another.

As the smoke wafted toward Albert, he tried not to gag on the overwhelming smell. "No."

"Can she make our plan come to fruition?"

Albert hoped this was her last question. "Our investigator assures us if anyone can do it, it's her. She's been a gifted racer since she was a child. She used to fake her age to race. She started when she was five years old. Her father was a mechanic of some sort." Speaking exhausted the breath he'd been holding in an attempt not to inhale any more of his mother's smoke. He was forced to take another breath of smoke-laden air.

His mother leaned back her head and laughed. "Spectacular!" She enunciated each syllable clearly. Her dark eyes locked with his.

"Albert, you know what to do. Make this happen—spare no expense. Get the best!"

She stopped while she took another life-sucking breath from her second cigarette.

"And, Albert, the cars will be fuchsia." Her eyes narrowed, her lips puckering to blow out a cloud of white billowing smoke, waiting, he was sure, to pounce on him if he answered incorrectly.

"Yes, Mother."

She leaned back with her usual wicked smile plastered on her face. "Oh, and, Albert?"

Rising to leave, he stopped. Wary of her tone, he didn't move. He sensed she could smell his fear and she silently celebrated producing it in him.

"Yes, Mother?"

"Do not screw this up or I will put you back in the mail room." She casually puffed on her cigarette.

"Yes, Mother … I mean, no, Mother, I won't." Albert quickly exited her office while he exhaled another breath he had been holding. He had work to do.

Chapter One

"This is by far the craziest thing you have ever thought of doing, Lee."

Lee turned his head from the track and met Darrin's annoyed stare.

"If I'm so crazy, engine man, why are you standing next to me looking at the same thing I am?" Lee yelled over the noise of the car engines revving and a few hundred people talking at once. They stood in the stands of Marigold Raceway, which was the pride of the small city, smack in the heart of the Montana countryside.

"Hell if I know. I guess I couldn't pass up the huge amount of money they offered me on this crazy scheme," Darrin shouted back.

"I guess you answered your own question."

"Well, folks, the event you have all been waiting for has finally arrived."

As the announcer finished his sentence, the speaker tweaked with feedback. Lee cringed, then placed his hands over his ears as the crowd groaned in complaint.

"Tonight we have a special treat, the main event, as Cass Jamison returns for the third year in a row to defend her title, taking pole position earlier tonight in the qualifying runs."

There was a roar from the crowd as the drivers walked to their vehicles. Lee watched a slim, baseball-capped fair-haired female driver throw a wave at the call of her name. She hopped into her 1969 modified Chevy Camaro stock car, strapping herself in for the ride.

She was the only female in the motley crew. This race was the pure stock car category; twenty laps around the asphalt track and anything goes. One step above the demolition derby category, Lee thought.

He knew the routine. When all the drivers were in place, they would pull on their helmets. After the announcement, they would start their engines.

Each was consulting with their crew before the final call of the race was made. The female he assumed was Cass was conferring with a young man with a baseball cap proudly displaying the sponsor's name. He was probably the mechanic or car owner. She was nodding her head, making signals with her hand.

"This should be interesting," Darrin noted.

Lee ignored him as he watched the field.

She is awfully small.

In slenderness, he amended, not height. From the top of the field, she appeared to compete in height with most of the men, probably around 5'7" or so. The announcer's voice drifted over the loudspeaker.

"Get ready, folks, and let's see if our little lady Cass can pull it off again this year."

Lee's excitement grew as the green flag was let loose and the cars surged forward with Cass in the lead. He watched in silence as he assessed the skills of the Lovely Cosmetics

NASCAR protégé. He smiled as the crowd shouted their approval as the twenty cars jockeyed for position around the field, rushing around the track lap after lap. He loved the sound of the track.

The excitement from the roar of these vehicles was second only to sex as far as he was concerned.

His grin turned to a frown as he saw Cass wasn't in the lead. Instead, she stuck to the leader's bumper like glue, more than likely drafting to gain more speed.

Dangerous.

She seemed to be keeping her position without much effort. It was almost as if she was purposely remaining in that position.

Ahhh, she has a plan.

Around and around they continued, amid the smell of rubber, the gasp of the crowd as cars banged together, and finally the roar of the engines, which drowned out all other noise.

Lee watched as Cass continued to closely follow the first position driver. He began to wonder if she would actually win the race. She should have made her move much sooner. As they rounded the last curve to the finish, Lee sucked in a stressed breath when she suddenly bolted alongside the number one driver, rubbing the side of her car against his. Her wheels were riding on the bottom side of the track, barely touching the dirt center.

She had placed herself in a very hazardous position. Too much wheel on the gravel and she could lose her grip on the track and spin out. Suddenly, she punched ahead and passed the other driver, then dropped in front of him an instant before the checkered flag declared her the winner.

Lee released the breath he had been holding without realizing it.

The crowd around him surged to their feet, screaming, clapping and chanting her name. She pulled onto the side pit area as her small crew surrounded her and lifted her out of the car, throwing her up into the air. They set her down long enough for her to pull off her helmet, allowing her long golden hair to cascade down her racing suit.

Lee's lips twitched in response to her radiant smile as she laughed with her crew. Even from a distance, her beauty was arresting, causing Lee to shift in his seat as he tried to adjust his erection. He heard Darrin shift next to him and mutter one word. "Incredible!"

Lee continued to watch the celebration and awards ceremony, trying to size up her potential. He suspected she had known exactly what she was doing when she passed the leader on the third curve.

He grinned. Maybe this wasn't such a crazy idea after all.

~

Cassandra grinned and waved to her crew as she walked to the parking lot where her motorcycle awaited. She was glowing with happiness. Her only disappointment was that her sister had been unable to see her win the title this year. She had finally packed Jewel up last week and driven her to the University of Washington in Seattle, where she had earned a full scholarship. Cass was so proud of her.

Racing like she did tonight was the pinnacle of her existence. Her need for speed and the thrill of the competition were like a drug to her, a sometimes dangerous habit. She'd felt this craving for racing since she was a small girl. It didn't matter what or who; she would race tricycles with the local neighbor boys.

She smiled as she made her way to her street bike, a sleek black Ninja model made, of course, for speed. She already felt the familiar tingle when she thought about taking the curves of the road.

"Cassandra Jamison?"

The sound of her name startled her and she stopped in mid-stride, warily watching two men walking toward her. She was suspicious as she always was with strangers.

"Who's asking?" She eyed them intently from head to toe when they stopped in front of her. There was a handsome older gray-haired man, the lines of character evident in his face. Next to him was a tall, skinny blond man, cute in a lanky way.

"May we have a minute of your time?"

She eyed the man who anxiously asked her the question. "Depends on what you want to waste it on." She gave him her most unfriendly expression, the one that usually told people to stay away from her, that she wasn't a woman to come on to. Guys were always hitting on her after races.

"Um." The man seemed taken aback with her demeanor.

Good, Cass thought, she was accomplishing just what she wanted to, a stay-away-from-me attitude.

"I'm Lee Gray, I'm here representing Lovely Cosmetics, and my company is interested in sponsoring you."

She felt a rush of anger. "Well, sorry for wasting your time, Mr. Gray, but I'm not interested in modeling. I consider the career a degrading profession for women." She swiveled on her boot heels and started to stride toward her bike.

"Um, Ms. Jamison, we weren't interested in you for modeling. We are interested in sponsoring you as a driver."

She stopped so fast her boots skidded on the gravel. She turned, not sure she had heard him right. She thought he had said they wanted her to drive for them.

"What?" Cass questioned the gray-haired man. The blond sidekick hadn't said anything, just stood there, looking uncomfortable.

"I'm a Team Manager, Ms. Jamison, this is my Chief Mechanic, Darrin Jacks. We represent Lovely Cosmetics and we want you to consider driving our NASCAR in the Nextel Cup this year, including Daytona."

Her jaw completely dropped and her mouth formed an O.

NASCAR. Daytona. Those were words she had only dreamed of hearing.

Then the name suddenly dawned on her. Lee Gray, the crew chief for the NASCAR Kid Justin Steed, who had claimed the Winston Cup Series five years in a row starting at the young age of eighteen. That was until he was injured in a near-fatal wreck in the last race of his sixth series.

"Lee Gray," she said the words out loud, "of the NASCAR Kid team?"

He stuck out his hand, smiling. "The one and only."

"Oh, my God." Cass placed her hand in his, too stunned to even comment after her initial shock. She transferred her hand to Mr. Jacks.

"I'm so sorry ... I didn't know ... I'm sorry if I was rude. You don't understand how many lewd offers I get after a race like this."

"That's okay, Ms. Jamison, we understand."

"Call me Cass. Are you guys crazy? A woman has never made it through the Nextel Cup Series. They have never been able to maintain steady sponsorship. Why do you think I can do it?"

"The question, Cass ... is do you think you can do it, and are you willing to try?"

Cass smiled at his question.

Lee stepped back. He was stunned at her appearance. She wasn't just beautiful; she was striking. Her ice blue eyes were the first feature that caught his attention, then the elegant lines of her face and nose followed by the most astonishing wavy golden mane of hair he had ever seen.

Up close and in person, she was breathtaking.

Then there was her smile, that devastating smile, one that could bring down an entire building, one that could sell anything. He couldn't help but smile in return.

"Boys, you've got yourself a driver."

She whooped and dropped her helmet, raising her hands in the air. Then she launched herself on both of them, laughing and hugging them until she almost knocked them over.

She is strong for a slight thing.

He and Darrin glanced at each other. Darrin, who Lee wasn't sure he had ever seen smile, had a quirk at the corners of his lips. He mouthed the word "women" to Lee as he was being squeezed in a bone-crushing hug. He didn't seem too uncomfortable. As a matter of fact, Lee saw Darrin's arms set around her in return, and watched in amazement as Darrin's lips stretched into a full smile.

He stepped forward and pulled Cass out of Darrin's arms. This one was dangerous and she didn't even know it.

Chapter Two

"Just watch her, Justin." Lee pleaded over the phone.

Justin sat on the hard stool in his kitchen. If it was anyone but Lee, he wouldn't waste his time listening. "We'll come down for a week," Lee continued, "and you can evaluate whether you can train her."

"Lee, you're crazy. A woman cannot complete with the men of this sport. I don't care how good she is, it's not possible."

"We've been here for a week and she's proven her skills in every situation we've thrown at her. She has what it takes. I can feel it. She has an instinct for the road, the car."

Lee paused. When he spoke again, his voice was impatient. "Besides, I'm authorized to offer you more money than you could imagine, and I know that horse ranch is sucking it up faster than you can make it."

Justin ran a hand through his tousled black hair. Lee was right. Justin wasn't making enough money from the hay and cattle from the ranch. He wasn't yet established enough in the horse stud business to get the time of day. He needed to hire some help, but couldn't afford it.

"All right, one week. If I don't like what I see, then she's out of here. Agreed?"

"Agreed, although I'm one hundred percent positive you'll like what you see." Justin heard Lee chuckle, and he became wary. He didn't like this one bit.

"Fine, see you in a few days," Justin commented.

"We're going to bring the cars with us so you can see her in them. It will be her first chance at running a real NASCAR on a genuine NASCAR track," Lee said enthusiastically.

Justin groaned. "Great, she hasn't even handled a NASCAR style stock car before."

"Hey, trust me. I have an eye for the best. I picked you, didn't I?"

Yeah, and look where I am now.

"Yeah, Lee, you did."

"Okay, see you in a few days. 'Bye." Lee rang off.

Justin put down the phone and remained stretched out on the kitchen barstool.

He fingered the scar on the side of his face. His fingers drifted down to the scar on his arm and finally, he rubbed his leg.

Right, look where it had gotten him, at twenty-seven his body broken and so desperate for money he was training a woman to possibly go through the same nightmare he had experienced. Broke, broke, and broke.

He ran a hand over his face, wincing. Hell, he wasn't going to sit here and feel sorry for himself. He shook his head and rose to take care of the horses.

He limped slightly going out the door, questioning his judgment. What the hell did he just agree to do?

~

Cass eased back on her bike and enjoyed the view.

Three days of traveling and they had crossed the state line heading toward their destination, Sterling, Arizona, a small town outside of Tucson, and the home of Justin Steed's ranch.

They would stay with Steed while he trained her in the art of driving a NASCAR at the Tucson Raceway.

She was so excited she couldn't sit still, which was why she had opted to ride her motorcycle somewhere between Idaho and Utah. She loved the feel of the wind against her body and the ability to view the scenery whizzing by uninhibited by car windows.

This is where I am comfortable, on the road.

She was following the trailer that held the two gaudy fuchsia NASCARs and her other dirt bike. God, she reflected, looking at the cars. If she weren't so excited to drive them she would almost be embarrassed.

She thought about Justin Steed, the yummy-attractive young NASCAR driver named the NASCAR Kid because he was only eighteen when he had won his first Daytona.

He was a gifted driver, well liked in the field. He had the ability to turn any situation into a win. He was a fox and that image drew in women and fans.

It had been three years since the near fatal accident at the Atlanta Motor Speedway that lost him the title and nearly cost him his life.

Cass remembered seeing the accident on TV. She had been seventeen and she'd always made an event out of watching the annual Winston Cup Series races with her father.

She had been terrified when she watched the twenty-four-year-old, five-year-in-a-row champion get wrenched out of his car and carried in a stretcher to the ambulance.

His body was clearly broken, blood running down his face. Besides occasional updates on his condition, she had never heard about him again. He would be twenty-seven now, and she had an insatiable curiosity to meet him. She was excited and at the same time anxious about this opportunity to be trained by the man who was held in such esteem by the NASCAR world.

~

Justin heard a car pull up in his dirt driveway and walked out to greet his guests. There was only one car and he was surprised when only Lee, Darrin and some of his support crew exited. As they approached him, Lee smiled and pushed out his hand.

"How are you, old man? Darrin?" Justin asked, clapping Lee on the back as he pumped their hands.

"So," he said, looking for a female in the group, "where's the star of this show?"

"Um." Lee rubbed his shadowed jaw and turned, and glanced toward the highway they had exited. It ran horizontal to the house with a vertical dirt road about a half-mile off leading to Justin's.

"She couldn't sit still in the car," he murmured, peering at the road. His face lit up and he lifted his hand, pointing to the trailer and the motorcycle following behind it.

"Ah, there she is."

Amazed, Justin gazed out to the freeway, watching the crazed motorcycle rider streak past the trailer, going faster than he could even calculate. When the rider approached the dirt road, the bike barely slowed. Leaning low to the side, the rider executed a perfect turn, careening onto the dirt road, rocks and dirt flying behind the bike as it sped toward Lee's parked car.

Suddenly, the bike screeched to a stop not five feet from them, dust flying, creating a halo around the rider. Flipping down the kickstand, Justin watched as the black leather-cloaked individual pulled off the full-face helmet.

Leaning down, the rider swung long, golden hair over her shoulders, revealing the most stunning woman Justin had ever laid eyes on. Her wavy blonde hair settled messily, sexily, to frame her perfectly formed face and luscious pink lips. Her cheeks held a touch of natural pink and those eyes, those mesmerizing ice blue eyes, were naturally framed with thick black lashes.

She wasn't wearing a stitch of makeup, Justin noticed. His eyes ran down her form-fitting leather suit to take in her slim well-formed body, the right amount of curves in the right places.

Pulling off her black leather riding gloves, she smiled. Reaching out a hand she greeted Justin. "Pleased to meet you."

Her honey-dipped, low sexy voice had Justin's breath caught in his throat, his cock standing to attention. He managed to get out one weak word, "Incredible."

Justin heard laughter behind him.

Cass studied the man before her. She'd always had a schoolgirl crush on this guy. On TV he was hot, but in person he was mind-blowing. Her heart began pounding in her chest like it did in the last five minutes of her fastest, most exciting race.

His short, tousled black hair was fashionably cut above his ears; his chiseled features were perfect except for the scar running the length of his right temple and fanning from his left eye. But the scar added to his rough attractiveness.

Good God, he is so sexy.

As she watched him, his dark brown bedroom eyes studied her back with unfathomed meaning. Her eyes slowly ran down his body as his did hers, returning the favor. His broad muscular shoulders and veined bare arms gave her a preview of what was underneath. His tight black Levi's didn't leave much to her imagination except that he was well endowed. He was tall, towering over her five-seven by at least five inches. He made her feel small and the way he was eating her up with his eyes definitely made her feel feminine.

Cass felt heat radiate from her face, down her body to her stomach, then trickle down to her vagina. She shook her head and cleared her throat, trying to get some semblance of control back into her thoughts. Sticking out her hand, she greeted him.

"Pleased to meet you," she said.

When his hand joined with hers, she felt instant heat, a tingling sensation, and a stunning attraction. Her eyes locked with his, and she immediately wondered what he would look like without all of those clothes and how he would feel if she ripped them off right there.

Cass shook her head; she couldn't believe her thoughts.

She had never experienced this kind of desire for a man before. Previously, the emotion she usually felt was the need to show them up on the raceway.

Her sexual dossier was fairly limited; a couple of fucked up relationships out of high school had soured her to the whole idea of sex. She never could see what all the fuss was about. She could give herself an orgasm by masturbation and not have to hassle with having a man around. All she wanted right now was to drive, and these emotions were in total contrast to her purpose.

Knock that crap off.

His hand squeezed hers so hard it almost hurt. She tried to tug it out of his, but he wouldn't release her.

"Are you out of your mind riding in here like that? You could have killed yourself. You could have killed us. That was reckless."

The pressure on her hand was becoming painful. Since he wouldn't release it, she decided to show him this was no way to treat a lady. Moving her other hand to his wrist, she applied pressure in a very sensitive, painful nerve at his wrist. His hand immediately opened. She pulled her hand out of his grasp and stepped back, taking a defensive posture, her legs apart.

"Try that again and I'll land that pretty ass right where you're standing," Cass threatened.

He reached out to capture her arm. He wanted to put her in her place, she guessed. She already knew her place: the winner's circle.

She stepped forward, hooked her considerably smaller leg behind his, and gave him a hearty shove. He toppled like a cut tree right onto, as she described, his pretty rear.

He sat there in the dirt and gravel and she had to laugh at the amazed expression on his face. Then he glared at her. Taking pity on him, she reached down her arm to help him up.

"Truce," she offered.

Justin narrowed his eyes. He wanted to strangle the woman. He reached up to grab her arm and, hooking his foot behind hers, he pulled her down into the dirt. She landed with an oomph noise right next to him, her hips touching his, her arm cradled in his hand. Where their bodies met, he felt heat. Not just a dry Arizona heat, it was a mind-tingling, fiery sexual slam to his equilibrium. It made him think of hot, sweaty sex.

He took a deep, cleansing breath and released her arm. Trying to shake off the need to strip her naked in his head, he smiled at her. Heaving himself off the ground he offered his hand to her. "Sure, truce."

Justin could tell she was fuming. Ignoring his hand, she struggled up on her own accord and approached him ready to do battle again.

Justin had never seen a woman so beautifully, fuming mad; sweat was glistening on her face from the smoldering heat and her leather prison. He backed up, smiling, as she stalked him. He couldn't help it; he discovered he was actually enjoying himself. There was a part of him that wanted to trip her again, but this time land directly on top of him to feel the pleasure of her body fully against his. The desire he had tried so hard to squelch kicked back up.

She was watching him. He was baiting her, and it made her even madder. She growled as she made a move to launch on him. They both stopped at the sound of Lee's voice.

"Justin Steed, meet Cassandra Jamison."

Cass coughed into her hand, as if to cover her embarrassment.

"Kids, if you're through rolling around in the dirt, can we get out of this heat and get this show on the road?"

Justin peered at Lee guiltily. Dropping the hands he was sure she was preparing to pummel him with, Cass started to remove her jacket. She appeared overheated. Justin stared at her. This was not going to be a warm and fuzzy relationship, he thought.

"For your information, I am never reckless. I am always in control," she said, then squared her shoulders and turned to follow Lee.

"We'll see about that, Ms. Jamison, we'll see."

She turned to glower at him.

He had gotten the last word in after all.

Chapter Three

Cass lay unsleeping in her bed. She had battled with Justin all night, his hostility open and biting. He criticized everything she did, everything she said. She was beginning to get the feeling he didn't like her. Lee had acted like a mediator throughout dinner, trying to soften Justin's demeanor and dreadfully failing.

Finally, frustrated with the whole situation, Cass announced that she was going to bed. After confirming when they wanted her the next morning, she walked off—well, more like huffed off—to her bedroom without even a good night. She heard Lee and Justin loudly arguing and finally a door slamming, which she assumed was Justin going to his own room.

Cass was starting to have serious doubts as to whether she could train with a man who disliked her so much. Wiping a tear from her eye, she growled in frustration. She wasn't usually prone to tears but the strain of the past few days had gotten to her. The endless driving, trying to impress Lee and Darrin. The three days of traveling through the heated dessert. But it had taken Justin's unending criticism to finally do her in and, regrettably, she did what most women did to relieve their stress. She cried.

Could she do NASCAR? What was she thinking, competing in a world dominated by men, where she wasn't welcome? More tears ran down her face. She had been handed everything she had ever dreamed of on a silver platter and now she distrusted herself.

Maybe she was reckless. Then again, maybe that's why she was so good at what she did. She angrily mopped the tears from her face and swung her legs off the bed.

She obviously wasn't going to get any sleep.

She decided to raid the kitchen. With Justin's constant questions and harping, she had hardly eaten at dinner.

She remembered his questions: *Why did she think she had what it took to race a NASCAR?*

She had answered because she was good at driving.

He had laughed and told her it took more than skill to race with the big boys and he doubted she had the balls. She had assured him she didn't have the balls but she did have the heart.

He had laughed again, mocking her.

Justin jerked up in bed, his breathing rapid, his heart pounding, sweat pouring down his body. For a minute he was disoriented, thinking he was still lying in his crushed car.

He ran his hand over his wet face.

He hadn't had a nightmare about the accident in months.

He swung his feet out of the bed and leaned down, pressing his face into his hands. It was that woman, her enthusiasm for racing and the spirit he saw in her eyes. She reminded him of himself at her age, and that was what probably scared him the most about her.

He had been hard on her tonight, berating her, trying to break her, taunting her into finally leaving the table. He felt guilty now when he contemplated how he had behaved. He had been trying to hurt her, he wanted her to leave; he wanted to tell her she was pursuing a sport that stared death right in the eye every time you crammed yourself behind the wheel of the car.

He wanted to scream it at her.

Instead he had beaten her with his words, with his sarcasm, and with his skepticism of her abilities.

He saw the hurt in her eyes every time he flung an insult her way, and he couldn't stop himself from doing it again. Now he was paying the price. Guilt ate away at his gut like late night heartburn, leaving him empty and remorseful. It wasn't his place to tell this woman how to run her life. It was his place to train her to the best of his abilities, to teach her how to cheat death.

He sighed and rose, then made his way to the kitchen. He heard scraping noises beyond the door and moved through it to investigate. Teetering on a chair, reaching for a glass, was the vision he had been berating himself about. And very scantily clad.

His eyes roamed down her shapely muscular legs to where the T-shirt had lifted enough to give him a glimpse of her ass. Her creamy skin and black lace thong panties made his cock rise.

"What are you doing?" he barked out, trying to replace his desire with anger.

She screeched, and swayed from side to side.

Oh great, she's going to fall.

He rushed forward, reaching out to catch her. She fell smack dab into his arms.

Caught by surprise, Cass jumped when she heard the voice behind her. All of a sudden, Cass' racing acuity completely flew out the window as she felt herself falling off the chair. But instead of hitting the cold hard floor, she landed against Justin Steed's naked wet chest and into his arms.

Her arms flew out and anchored around his neck. Her blue eyes flew to his warm brown ones, and strayed down to the wall of his well-muscled almost hairless chest.

Oh God.

Her sleeping shirt had ridden up, exposing a good deal of her naked thigh. Guiltily her gaze left his hard chest to return to his face.

She saw something in his eyes besides anger this time. The color had deepened from brown to black, smoky black. She saw his gaze stray to her exposed thigh. Beneath her hand, she felt his pulse accelerate. He shifted her in his arms and she tightened her hold on his neck.

She shivered as he continued to stare at her, his eyes trailing from her thigh to the vee of her shirt. During her fall, two of the three buttons opened, exposing a considerable amount of her cleavage. Cass felt an urgent need to lean closer and draw his face to hers. To feel those sensual lips exhale against hers. She could smell his scent, a masculine musky smell. His hair was wet and sweat dotted his chest, as if he had been working out or awakened from a bad nightmare.

Everything about him intrigued her: his scarred face, those bedroom brown eyes, and that tousled black hair, like he had been running his hands through it. No man had ever evoked the burning desire in her that this man seemed to stir, even in the short time she had known him. None had made her want to lick them from head to toe, like he did.

In her fantasies she didn't want a gentle seduction, she wanted a rough one, and she was sure that this man didn't have a gentle bone in his body.

Making love with him would be intense.

Her stomach clenched and she felt a flow of juices radiate between her thighs from her pussy. She licked her lips in anticipation and without thinking the hands anchored to his neck opened and begin inching slowly up, delving into his hair.

She heard his involuntarily groan and watched his eyes close for a second. They snapped back open. The desire she thought she had seen was gone, replaced by the familiar narrowing, one she was starting to recognize as anger.

He released her so quickly she had to grab his wide shoulders in an attempt to balance herself. Once she stood on her own, she jerked away from him. She whirled from him to the sink and started filling the tea kettle she had found on the stove. Her hand trembling, she turned off the faucet and put the kettle on the stove.

Neither spoke of the incident.

He remained standing in the middle of the kitchen, as if he wasn't sure which way to go, in or out. He must have opted for in because he moved over to bar and sank down into the chair. She noticed for the first time that he walked with a slight limp, no doubt a remnant of his accident.

Justin was at a loss for words. Holding her barely clothed body against his naked chest had sent his brain spiraling to areas he had no business going. Like wondering what would happen if he pulled her against him and ravished her lips under his.

As his eyes had run down her body, questions kept popping up in his mind: What would her naked body feel like with her bare breasts rubbing against his chest? What would her nipples taste like? Would her pussy be as hot and tight as he sensed it would be?

He had completely lost control of his thoughts, and wasn't helped any by her response, her hands moving up his neck to bury her fingers in his hair. He shook his head. What was he thinking? She was a child, a twenty-one year old girl, and these thoughts of raw sex had to stop.

I'm supposed to be her trainer, for God's sake.

"You don't like me much, do you, Justin?"

He cringed with guilt and remained silent, not sure what to say. He heard a slam and his head jerked up.

She banged the kettle on the stove and turned to confront him.

"Look, Steed!"

Uh oh, she's not using my first name any more.

"If you don't trust me or my abilities, if we can't reach some sort of truce here, then I suggest I go get dressed, hop on my bike and get the hell out of here. Because at this point it seems I don't like you any more than you like me." She pointed to him then back at herself. "There needs to be complete trust between us. You hold my life in your hands at the other end of that Com. If you're not up for this ride then I suggest we end this relationship. Right now!" She made a slashing motion with her hand. "I'll find someone else to train me because I will do this, with or without your help." She crossed her arms in front of her in a defensive posture.

He remained silent. He hadn't meant to do this, to drive her away to another trainer. Or had he? He had just thought if he pushed her she might re-think this crazy idea of racing a NASCAR.

She swung back and turned off the stove, then she strode out of the room with a parting remark. "If that's the way you want it, fine with me."

Surely she won't leave right now.
Then he thought about the woman he had learned she was, fearless, reckless, and strong.

He vaulted off the bench to follow her. He found her in her room shoving a few clothes into a backpack. She had pulled on her black leather riding pants and it appeared she was preparing to leave.

"Unless you want to see me naked I suggest you turn around." Justin leaned back against the door jamb. Crossing his arms, he let his body language tell her he wasn't going anywhere.

She shrugged and ripped her nightshirt off. He received a quick glance of her perfectly formed breasts and dark brown nipples before she put on a tight riding shirt. Her pants were unbuttoned, showing a good amount of her skimpy lace thong before she tucked in her shirt.

Justin shifted as he felt his blood move through his body and center in his penis. She was so gorgeous; she stirred him to hardness with a simple glimpse of her breasts. She sat on the bed and began putting on her socks and boots. He uncrossed his arms.

She can't leave.
She laced up her boots and stood.
"Tell Lee I'll send for the rest of my things later."
Grabbing her helmet, she started for the door. He stepped up to block her exit.

"Cass, you can't leave. It's the middle of the night. It's dark out."

She shrugged at his comment and attempted to shimmy around him. He grabbed her arm.

"Don't," he said in a low voice.

That one word stopped Cass. She looked from the hand on her arm into his eyes. She continued to stare at him, daring him to go further.

"Don't go," he commanded again.

"Why? Give me one good reason I shouldn't walk out of here right now? And don't give me this crap about it being dark and late, because I think you know I'm an experienced enough rider to make my way in the dark."

He nodded, giving her one small victory.

"Because..." he paused.

She watched him warily, waiting for his answer.

"I want you here." His hand moved to her face. He so gently, so softly, caressed her cheek. Then his arm dropped, and it was almost as if he hadn't touched her at all.

Cass did a double take.

Just like that.

Because he wants me here.

Those simple words meant so much to her. They shouldn't have, but they erased the negative hurtful ones he had hurled at her all evening.

Her gaze drifted to his eyes, darting over his face searching for the sarcasm, trying to find the anger she'd suffered from all night.

There was none.

What she saw was sincerity. His touch had soothed her resentment, a powerful, compelling appeal for her to stay.

By now she had learned when it came to words this man wasn't eloquent. The ones he had chosen tonight, even unspoken, began an unsaid truce between them.

"How did you become a race car driver anyway?" he asked.

She smiled. "My father had pieced together my first motorcycle when I was five. He constructed it from scratch. Racing is in my blood."

"Tell me." He shifted even closer to her. She could almost taste the warmth of his body radiating off of him like a furnace. It was a heady feeling. His nearness made her thoughts drift to indecent ones.

"My mother was a driver. I eventually went from motorcycles to cars."

"Ahhh, now it all makes sense. A race car baby." She nodded at his accurate assessment.

He reached down and joined their hands, the way one might do when making a pact with a best friend. She felt the heat radiate from their clasped hands up her arm and centering in her stomach. His touch was soothing and hot at the same time—making her think of sexy hot summer nights in Las Vegas.

Oh God, here I go again.

"Partners," he simply said.

She nodded because she couldn't find her voice.

"Partners," she confirmed finally. And then she smiled.

"You better get some rest. Tomorrow we determine if you've got what it takes to race a NASCAR in the simulator." He returned her smile and for the first time since she met him, she felt he had come to terms with their relationship and her role in it.

"Oh, I know I have what it takes and believe me, by the end of the day so will you."

Chapter Four

Justin tucked Cass' hair into her fire cover that rested on her head. It was a simple gesture, one a husband might do, but it sent a thrill shivering through her. She stood next to the gaudy, sticker-ridden, sponsor-identified, fuchsia NASCAR. He had a headset attached to his head, the one they had affectionately termed the Com. His sunglasses blocked his eyes from hers.

He looked sexy as usual. Momentarily distracted, Cass licked her lips, wishing he were a Popsicle and she was licking him right now.

He leaned down. "Remember what I told you," he said, his lips so close to her ear she felt the puff of his warm breath. "This isn't a stock car. It has much more power than anything you've ever handled and the gearing will be lower."

"We've gone over this a hundred times. I did fine in the simulator, let me get into the car." The stress of three long days of virtual practicing sharpened her voice.

"Okay, do it!"

She lifted her right leg, her hands on the car frame, and with Justin's help shimmied into the custom fit seat. Her rear rested on the window frame. She pulled the other leg and carefully guided her body through the opening and into the cockpit.

The first thing Cass noticed was the grip of the seat. It wasn't fancy and not even very comfortable. The aluminum structure engulfed her body. The side panel cupped her legs, curving inward to her ribcage, and her legs stretched out nearly straight. Her head was encased by the safety wrap-around headrest.

Justin handed the helmet to and helped her lock into the five-point safety harness. He pulled it, testing its strength. It's definitely tight and unforgiving, she thought. She was sure she would feel the pain from the grip in the morning.

She tugged on the straps, as Justin had, to prove to herself they were tight. She definitely didn't want to come out of the seat in the event of an accident.

Justin snapped the steering wheel into place on the column protruding through the dashboard. Cass pulled on her full-face helmet, reached over and hooked up her speaker and other various attachments: her fresh air blower, radio wires, Gatorade tube.

Cass peered around the car. It was a tight fit. Roll bars, a somewhat comforting visual, surrounded her. She sat in a protective cocoon that she hoped she would never have to test, ever.

Various people milled around the car preparing it. One was removing the vinyl cover of the windshield, another disconnecting the oil tank heater. She was now strapped into a 358-cubic foot engine, 750-horse and 3,400 pounds of pure power. Justin gave her a thumbs up signal, snapped the window net into place, then left to stand outside the raceway in the traditional area of the crew chief.

He stepped back onto the side of the track and she heard his sexy voice in her ear.

"Test, test, Cass are you reading?"

"Yes, loud and clear," she said into the microphone in front of her mouth. "Are you reading me?"

"Yes."

"Lee?" Cass questioned.

"Yes, I'm here too, next to Justin."

She gave Lee a wave and he returned it.

"Can you do something with this guy's personality, like a brain transplant." She watched him put his hands in the air in surrender.

"Funny." She heard Justin's voice again.

"Remember..." he began.

She cut him off. "Justin, let me do my job and you do yours, okay?"

"You're clear," Justin instructed, "crank it up."

Although she could no longer see him, she heard him. She was more frightened than she had ever been in her life, and knowing he was there gave her a sense of calm.

Cass flipped the ignition switch and the engine roared to life. She looked down and checked her gauges: water temperature, oil pressure, and tachometer.

Everything was good.

She eased down the clutch and slipped the car into first gear, her excitement mounting with each movement. Pressing the accelerator, she mapped her path and released the clutch and brake. The she slammed down on the accelerator and she was off.

The power, the pull and the exhilaration of the car under her sent her whooping for joy, and the race, for her, was on.

Second gear onto the straightaway, third gear going into the turn, the g-forces on the car pulling her toward the wall, then those same forces yanking her body toward the passenger side of the car as she grabbed fourth and exited turn two.

Both gloved hands gripped the trembling wheel. The power of the car shook the whole frame and it was a heady feeling.

I was born to do this.

She rounded the fourth curve heading for the front stretch. This was what she had dreamed of. She needed to get a feel for the car and the track. The best way to do that was to run at full throttle, otherwise she wouldn't get a real sense for what she was up against. She suddenly wanted to beat the odds—the first woman to make it in the series. She could almost taste it.

Justin expected her to slowly ease the car onto the track. He was staggered when she screeched away from her starting point and went screaming down the track. He heard her yell and eased the earpiece away from his head. He pulled it back on and spoke into the headphone. "Back off Cass," he instructed.

He didn't hear a response as she expertly negotiated the first turn. Picking up speed, she handled the car as if she'd been behind the wheel her whole life. Justin removed his glasses and shaded his eyes as he watched her fly around the curve heading to the backstretch.

He repeated his command. "Cass, ease off. You're only getting a feel for the car."

Justin was convinced she was ignoring the voice in her ear as she concentrated on the car and the track. In her total focus, she probably didn't hear his voice. He knew she was now in her world and there was nothing that could distract her.

It was just her, that car and the track; he remembered that feeling well.

Justin was concerned when she didn't slow down. Watching her speed increase, he began to plead in her ear. "Cass, you're burning needless tire. Back off."

He glanced at Lee who shrugged with a look that Justin knew well. It said *you're the crew chief, control your driver*. Justin was beginning to appreciate the role Lee had taken with him.

"Not easy to control them, is it?" Lee said, confirming Justin's thoughts.

He cringed. He'd never given a thought to how hard it was to be on this side of the speedway.

Cass flew by. Lee clicked on the stopwatch and showed Justin her time. He did a double take on the numbers.

"Wow," he said, confirming the numbers. She had driven a lap that competed with Justin's best NASCAR qualifying time.

"She has what it takes Justin, I can feel it." Lee's eyes followed her around her second lap as she moved back and forth, caressing the track, obviously trying to get a feel of it from all angles.

"Cass, back off." Justin's voice was urgent as he tried to reach her.

She completed another record lap time and continued.

Justin remembered the first time he had hooked up to a radio and knew she was in a zone where it was only her and the car. He needed to bust into that zone.

His role in her racing world was essential as he updated her on her laps and informed her of road conditions and driver placement. The person on the Com was critical to a successful NASCAR driver. He tried a different tactic; he gentled his voice, lowering it, taking on a sleepy tone.

"Cass, talk to me."

Cass was caught up in the intensity of the drive, the power of the car, concentrating on negotiating the curves, moving the car back and forth from the top of the track to almost the bottom line to get a feel for the track.

Suddenly Justin's purring voice penetrated her driving fog and her attention faltered. His warm, low voice caught her off guard and at his command she eased her foot off the accelerator. That voice made her think of a bear rug, a warm fire, a cold night and naked bodies entwined, preferably theirs. The car jerked slightly.

"Easy, Cass, get used to the sound of my voice. Don't lose your concentration, keep your line."

Yeah, right.

The way he said *easy* set her heart beating sharper than it already was. Almost like he was soothing a nervous filly.

She shook her head and tried to concentrate on her driving with his warm voice surrounding her.

"Back off a little and try to mingle my voice with your reactions."

She jolted at his comment, and the car jerked precariously. Her heart stopped beating for a second. One wrong move and this over-responsive car could skid and send her into a flip or something worse.

"Easy," his low voice calmed her. "Easy does it, okay?" Justin kept the tension he felt out of his voice as he watched the car shift around. He knew she was in a dangerous situation. He recognized she heard him now, and it was distracting her. She had slowed down some and seemed to be struggling to control the car.

"Okay?" he asked, hoping he could get her to take the next step and respond. He waited, watching her, praying she would leap this huge hurdle.

"Okay."

He let out the breath he had been holding. Her voice was magic when she answered him.

"Damn distracting, isn't it?" he asked, humor in his voice, trying to lighten the pressure he knew she felt.

"Very." He heard her strained voice over the other end. For some reason he so badly wanted to hold her right now, to reassure her that she was going to make it through this. Strange, he thought, that he continued to feel this unwanted, undeniable attraction to her.

"It will get better, listen and try to adjust to my voice. I'm going to give you feedback on the track. What to look for, like we would in a race."

"Okay," she said, her voice starting to sound more confident as she eased the accelerator back up and continued to circle the track.

It was a long and frustrating day as Cass battled with Justin, attempting to assimilate his voice and follow his instructions. He knew he was telling her to ease off when she wanted to move forward, to apply brakes when she wanted to apply accelerator. He knew the heat was affecting her, experienced first hand that water that was dripping down her back like a leaking faucet. He tested her abilities in every way.

They clashed, they argued, but in the end Cass delivered a racing performance that rivaled the best in NASCAR and grudgingly won Justin's respect. He was sure he, in turn, earned hers. In an unspoken agreement between Justin and Lee, it was decided that Justin would remain her crew chief.

~

"Pull her in, Cass. Let's call it quits for the evening."

She acknowledged Justin as she eased the car into pit row. She was surprised to see the sun lowering on the horizon. She had driven all day. She removed her helmet with a sigh of relief, and maneuvered out the window of the car.

She was hot and tired; the heat of Arizona in September had left sweat rings in her racing suit.

Justin approached as she exited the car and pulled off her fire hood. She took a deep breath, and suddenly she felt dizzy. She leaned her hand against the top of the car door, trying to lower the rapid beating of her heart, willing it to pass.

She closed her eyes, the heat pushing down on her, making her body slow and heavy, as if an anvil had been placed on her head. Propping her gloved hand against the door, she felt a hand on her shoulder and Justin's voice flowed against her ear.

"What's wrong?" The concern in his voice had her shaking her head.

"Nothing," she told him. Sliding her hand off the car, she attempted to pluck off her gloves. She swayed and felt Justin's arms curve around her, holding her up.

"Cass, never lie to me about your physical condition. It's critical that I be able to assess your ability to drive." His arms locked on hers.

She sighed. Even in her weakened condition she couldn't deny the heady feeling she felt resting in this man's arms.

"It's nothing. I'm not used to the heat. I imagine I'm a little dehydrated. Let me be." She tried to shake off his hold. "I need to get used to the feeling. I'm sure it won't be the last. Back off and let me deal with it." Her voice rose. "You know what it feels like."

He released her. She braced her hand against the car and steadied herself. Bending forward, she breathed in deeply, willing the dizziness to go away. She heard Lee approach, and felt a hand on her shoulder. Even before she glanced around, she knew it was Justin and not Lee. He held out a water bottle to her almost as if he was handing her an olive branch. Feeling better already, she straightened and accepted the water and slowly sipped it.

"Okay, I'm all right. Let's go." She started to peel off her racing suit. She was wet down to the bone with her own sweat. "I'm ready for a shower," she said, peeling the suit down to her waist.

Justin couldn't help noticing her healthy breasts outlined by her wet sports bra. He realized at a time like this she wasn't concerned about modesty but those breasts were damn distracting. Despite the heat, her nipples were standing out, teasing him. He shook his head, trying to clear his arousal.

They climbed into Justin's jeep to head back to the house. Cass had gone very quiet.

"You did good today..." He turned in the passenger seat and saw that her head was laid back against the seat, her eyes closed and she was unresponsive. He felt a spike of concern.

She was either asleep or simply out cold from exhaustion.

Justin moved to the back seat and laid a hand on her forehead.

She didn't respond.

She was burning up. He let his hand travel down her cheek and rested it on the pulse at her neck.

Good, it's slow and steady.

He tracked the rise and fall of her chest. She was breathing normally, just sleeping. He stared at her longer than necessary, his hand opening on her neck.

Her skin was so soft, so creamy, so different than his dark, calloused, worn hands. He ran his thumb along her classically lined jaw. Even in sleep she stirred something protective in him. She moaned and shifted at his caress, and he removed his hand before she woke. His cock was straining against his pants.

Christ, I'm in trouble.

Lee arrived, jumping into the driver's side of the jeep.

Justin pulled back from Cass. "I'm worried she can't handle it physically," he said as he climbed back into his seat. "You know, the main reason women have a hard time making it on the circuit is primarily sponsorship problems. Why should a sponsor take a risk on a female when they can have their male counterpart? Sometimes cockpit temperatures reach as high as 130 degrees. I'm not being sexist, but a man's built to handle it better than a woman."

"Justin, you were the same way when I trained you. Did you forget you used to fall asleep in the most unusual places?"

Justin laughed, remembering the times when, after a marathon training session, he fell asleep sitting straight up at the dinner table.

"Yeah." He smiled. "I guess you're right."

"Don't worry. She'll adjust. Dump her into a cool shower when we get back and she'll revive."

Justin turned and eyed Cass. Her dark lashes were fanned against her face, her sweat-streaked hair matted, yet still beautiful. Her breathing was rapid now and her head lolled when Lee turned onto the dirt road that led to his house.

"She is stunning," Justin murmured.

"Yes, she is," Lee agreed. "You're drawn to her, aren't you?"

Justin made eye contact with Lee, giving him a message not to go there.

Lee shrugged but didn't push for an answer. "Be careful."

"I know." Justin rubbed a hand on his neck and stared at her, wanting her, and mad at himself because he did. "I know."

Chapter Five

Cass was dreaming, floating, she was flying—yet she felt strangely safe. She wondered if this was a dream, and cracked her eyes open.

"Oh!" Cass exclaimed as she felt Justin's arms around her. He was carrying her down the hall to the bedroom.

"So, Sleeping Beauty finally awakens," he murmured as they approached her room.

Sighing, she burrowed into his arms. His arms were becoming a dangerous place to be. It was too warm, too comfortable, and much too stimulating.

He set her down on her bed and she made an effort to rise. His hand pressed against her shoulders, forcing her to stay down.

"Take about thirty minutes to rest, then you can get on the move again."

She took his advice and relaxed against his hand, still warm on her shoulder. She leaned her head up. He drew back his hand as if he had been stung and folded himself into the chair across from her.

"Make sure you take a cool shower when you feel rested enough and drink lots of water tonight. Tomorrow the rest of the crew is arriving and we'll be working on some mock racing with the other car and practicing your pit stops."

She leaned back and examined him. Her attraction to him increased daily. His virility appealed to her. He emitted an aura of action, even sitting in the chair now, and he seemed to vibrate with power. She sensed he wasn't at ease idle. He was like a caged lion wanting to be free. Free to do the one thing he could no longer do, she thought—race.

His graciousness about being a star had made him a hero and role model for adults and children alike. He frequently did public service announcements—for free, she'd heard—asking kids to stay in school and stay off drugs. He was admired by many, and feared only by his fellow drivers. Women flocked to him like sheep, attractive to his compelling persona.

He eased back in the chair as if agreeing to allow her to appease her curiosity about him. He was wearing a form-fitting tank top and shorts. The lined muscles of his arms bulged and his well-muscled tanned legs relaxed as he stretched them out in front of him, crossing his ankles over each other in an attempt to look casual.

Cass knew better.

His shirt clung with sweat to his frame, outlining his well-muscled stomach. The wariness in his eyes warned her not to go too far with her inspection. His scars showed lighter against his golden brown skin; on his arm, one running the length of his leg, and of course, the line on his face.

An unknown force pulled her to him. Cass rolled off the bed and gingerly approached him. His eyes narrowed, as if he was assessing her actions. She cautiously reached out her hand, touching the scar on his leg.

He jerked his leg away from her hand like a wounded animal injured in a snare. His hand snatched hers. He squeezed her fingers, hard.

He sat up in the chair and yanked away from her. He didn't say anything. Her eyes met with his and she attempted to tell him with her expression she wasn't going to hurt him. He released her hand.

Her fingers returned to their explorations, climbing, skimming the jagged scar on his arm. It was rough in a smooth way; the damaged texture intrigued her. Her entire being was caught up in the feel of his skin under her fingers. He leaned his head back and stared at the ceiling as if he was trying to regain control or pray. She wasn't sure which. She loved the touch of his skin, hot and smooth, lined with the scars of life, and the test of time.

I could become addicted to this sensation.

"I watched this." As if of its own volition, her hand continued caressing the scar on his arm.

His head jerked back down and his eyes clashed with hers. Her hand traveled from his arm to finger the scar on his face. At first he pulled back slightly. But she spoke again, and at the sound of her voice he stilled, seemingly mesmerized. She yearned to heal him.

"I was seventeen. It was the year before my parents died." He frowned at her comment. She continued, "My Dad and I always made an event of watching the Winston Cup races. When I saw the accident, my heart stopped beating in my chest. Then I saw you, after they had taken you out of the car." Dropping her hand, she shook her head. Remembering her horror on that day.

"I cried for you then." She laughed shakily. "Isn't that strange? I didn't even know you but I cried for you, for your pain, for the hero gone, for the career I knew had ended at that moment. And I prayed."

Tears formed in her eyes now and she swallowed. "I prayed not only for you, but that when I was in your place I wouldn't end up like that, stretched out, broken and beaten by the track. Because, in my heart I know it can happen, like that." She snapped her fingers. "In an instant. For the first time in my life I felt fear from my dreams of becoming like you. Longing to win so badly it could take my life away."

He leaned forward as if enthralled with her words. He locked his hand behind her head and drew her close to his face, so close her breath hitched.

Surely he's not going to kiss me.

"Good. Remember that fear, remember that feeling. Because when you are out there on that track I want you to taste that fear and maybe it will save your life some day."

She shook her head. "I can't." She gazed into his suffering eyes. "I can't drive that way. I have to drive without emotions. I have to forget those fears, otherwise they will drive me."

His laughter came out tortured. He roughly forced her hand to his leg and ran it over his embedded, rough scar. For a quick moment he closed his eyes, then opened them again and gave her an agonized glare.

"Remember this," he said.

Cass jerked her hand from his leg to deny him the satisfaction of knowing he had turned the tables and was frightening her.

She inched her lips closer to his. At the last second, she shifted past his lips to the scar at the side of his face. She placed a gentle kiss to his scar. His breath hitched. The hand locked on her neck moved into her mass of disheveled hair. She could smell him, a combination of sweat and the scents of the ranch. A unique combination of yummy flavors embedded into her brain.

"You're playing with fire, little girl." He snatched her head back so that their lips were aligned.

"Oh, but I'm reckless, remember? And you don't scare me," she whispered, her lips inching closer to his until her lips were a breath away from his. His lips were smooth and plump, and covered with Chapstick. They looked—well, they looked kissable.

"Cass, this isn't a good idea."

At this moment, she didn't care about it being good or bad. She only cared about feeling those sensual lips against hers, his breath exhaling against her lips. She wanted to kiss him so bad she could taste it.

She licked her lips in anticipation; a naive action from an inexperienced woman. These emotions were so foreign—a confused jumble took over her head. Her body ached with sensations. She wanted to feel him, to be close to him.

"I know," she agreed. "Not a good idea at all."

As if he couldn't hold onto his argument any longer, the hand in her hair jerked her head the last millimeter to his lips. The kiss was hard, fast, and rough, like the man, just like she expected.

This man doesn't do anything the slow and easy way, Cass thought.

His lips slanted against hers, opening her, drawing her into him. The hand in her hair anchored her head tightly against him, as if he was afraid that she would draw back.

Cass wasn't pulling anywhere but into the depths of his lips. Tentatively, innocently, her tongue strayed, exploring the recess of his mouth. She wanted to taste, to take, to have.

Groaning, he tensed the hand in her hair. His other hand flattened against her back, tugging her closer; she pressed against his chest. His position on the chair held her away from him. His tongue came out to dance with hers and he angled his head more to get closer to her lips.

Suddenly, he jerked back. His eyes were clouded, half lowered with desire and longing … and maybe a little surprise at her responsiveness.

Reaching forward, Cass grabbed his shoulders and wrenched him to his feet so that their bodies could get closer. Both of his arms curved around her, locking her body to his. His hands strayed, sinking to her ass. Bending his knees, he rubbed his aroused cock against her. Cass lost touch with reality; she could feel his hard penis against her belly and was assaulted with a need stronger than she had ever had. She had no doubt of his desire for her.

I want to own him.

He walked her backwardds and pushed her against the wall so he could get better leverage. Cass struck the wall with a grunt, air forced out of her lungs.

As if he realized how rough he'd gotten, he froze.

Dropping his arms, he released her like he'd been burnt and took two steps back. She watched him run a shaky hand through his dark hair.

"I told you, you were playing with fire, Cass. I don't do anything gently, including this. You need to go find someone your own speed." He took another step back, the back of his legs hitting against her bed.

She had a feeling he was thinking the more distance he put between them the easier it would be to stay away from her.

Her fervor grew.

Making love with this man would be like driving the wildest, most exciting track.

Her heart beat in anticipation.

She stepped to him. He watched her every move, his eyes hooded, hiding his emotion. She placed a hand in the middle of his chest. His heart was racing as fast as hers. He was gulping for air as if he'd run a fast race.

He is not unaffected by our kiss.

"Actually…" She ran her hand up his muscled chest, thrilled by the widening of his eyes. Reaching up, standing on her toes, she roughly delved her hand into his dark hair, pulling on it so he cried out in surprise. She crushed her mouth to his in a forceful, long kiss. Only then did she release his hair and pull back slightly. The thrill of knowing he was surprised by her assertiveness made her smile. There was a certain thrill in surprising a man at his own game. "…you're a little too slow for me."

He moaned, hauling her against him. Then his mouth claimed hers, deeper, expertly replacing her surprised, inexperienced kiss. Now she realized she had been way out of her league trying to fool this man.

He released her as suddenly as he had grabbed her, then stepped around her toward the door. Out loud, he cursed himself for his lack of control. As an afterthought, he turned.

"Be ready by 6:00 a.m. tomorrow." He left as unexpectedly as he had kissed her, shimmying out of the room faster than a race car running toward the checkered flag.

Cass swore at his departure. Falling onto the bed, she slugged her pillow. Laying her head down, she closed her eyes and promptly fell asleep, dirt, sweat and tangled hair intact.

Lee attempted to wake her later that evening to get something to eat. Her cries for him to leave her alone had him departing the room as quickly as Justin had.

She sure had a way of driving men away.

At one point, she sensed Justin coming in and watching her. Her eyes opened. She saw him sitting in the same chair he'd vacated earlier, but knew she must be dreaming. Her eyes closed, and she fell back asleep.

Later that evening when the house was quiet, Cass woke. She felt as if she was being watched. The first thing she did was look at the chair, but no one was there. She averted her eyes. Deciding she couldn't stand the feel of herself any longer, she arose and showered. She drank some more water. Wracked with exhaustion, she fell onto the bed again and went back to sleep.

Chapter Six

Voices and the smell of coffee had Cass springing up the next morning at 5:45 a.m. She raced around the room tugging on the shorts and tank top she'd wear under her race suit. Heeding Justin's warning to be ready, she hurried down the hall, pushing back her hair.

She peeled around the corner and ran straight into a large barrier. Hearing an *oomph*, she felt Justin's hand fall to her waist to steady her. When his hand came in contact with her flesh, he immediately pulled away.

"Hey, slow down, girl." His other hand held a cup of coffee that he was precariously trying to right.

"Not my style to go slow, Kid," she drawled, smiling at the shocked look on his face. He had gathered exactly what her double *entendre* meant. He moved away from her and dropped down to the kitchen table. Looking at the two dirty plates, she realized he and Lee had eaten already.

Lee was dishing up a full plate of eggs, bacon and hash browns for her. She accepted the plate with enthusiasm. Sitting at the table, she dug in. She'd missed dinner and knew she would need the energy. She thanked Lee as he handed her a glass of water.

"What, no coffee?" Justin asked.

"Nope, makes me nervous." She decided to ignore him. He was a constant distraction and she needed to focus on racing. Even bleary-eyed he was sexy as hell. He was wearing shorts and a skimpy shirt again that showed his muscled, bare flesh. The sight teased her, reminding her of how it felt to run her hands over that sculptured chest, her fingers grazing his scarred skin, his erection pushing against the softness of her stomach.

She finished eating and stood, nervous energy pumping through her system. She had to find something to stop her from thinking about Justin. It was obvious from his departure last night that he wasn't interested in her romantically.

"Let's go," she said, downing the rest of her water.

"I haven't finished my coffee. Would you take a breath?" He gave her his irritated expression.

"Meet you at the track then." Cass started to leave the kitchen. A hand on her arm stopped her, and she heard Lee clear his throat at Justin's action.

"You'll go with us." Justin's voice was steel. "You'll be exhausted tonight, in no shape to drive back." He applied pressure to her arm to make his point.

She felt anger rise inside her. From the beginning this man had assumed he could control her, and now she couldn't get him out of her head. She flipped her hair and jerked her arm out of his grasp.

"I haven't had a mother for quite a while." She lifted her chin. She sounded like a child, but she was so edgy, reliving that kiss, dreaming about his naked body. She needed to get away from him or she didn't know what she would do.

Justin took a step back and watched Cass. He saw the anger on her face, he could smell it, and he didn't believe it was because she wanted to go to the track. It was because of what happened last night. He shouldn't have given in to his overwhelming passion and touched her.

Then it dawned on him. She wasn't fuming because he had walked away from her last night, but because he was controlling her life and calling the shots.

She resented it.

This independent fierce woman was furious because she prided herself on remaining in control of her life and he was threatening that. He even glimpsed a little fear in her eyes, as if she were afraid to trust him completely. Her focus was on winning and his was on getting the ranch back into shape. It would be best if he didn't forget their goals.

Fear and anger were a heady combination on Cass. Her eyes were flashing, her soft lips were parted, her face flushed. With her emotions high she was spectacular. Justin was so drawn to her. He wanted to toss her onto the kitchen floor and bury himself inside of her.

He raised his hands in a signal of surrender and set his cup on the table.

Remember your goals.

"Okay, we'll go." By the tense expression on her face he knew he hadn't appeased her.

"Fine," she snapped.

"Fine," he repeated and flipped his hand, indicating for her to proceed.

She flounced out of the room. He turned, and Lee shrugged his shoulders as usual.

"I'll meet you at the track," Justin said. "Pick up the crew at the hotel. By the way, who did you get to drive backup?" He paused, waiting for an answer.

"Carmichael." Lee hesitated, as if waiting for the explosion.

"Brody?" Justin yelled, ignoring Lee's cringe. "Great, that's a problem waiting to happen, especially in the mood she's been in lately." Frustrated, he ran a hand through his hair.

"What mood?" Lee questioned.

Picturing Brody Carmichael, with his youthful rogue attractiveness, meeting Cass, with her compelling sensuality, Justin groaned. Brody was known for charming the ladies, for getting the girl. That's all he needed.

"Never mind, I'll see you at the track." He hurried to catch up with Cass before she got too impatient and left without him.

~

"Ooooh, now *that* is more like it."

Justin heard Cass' throaty exclamation as Brody Carmichael approached them on the track. The sweltering heat of the Arizona sun was beating down on him, irritating him, like Cass' sexy smile. He experienced an immediate disturbance in his chest, a constricted feeling he recognized as jealousy. Cass stepped forward, a mischievous smile on her face. He could swear she was acting like she was attracted to Brody on purpose to irritate him.

"Kid." Brody's Texas drawl surfaced and he shook Justin's hand. Releasing his hand, Brody turned toward Cass.

"Ma'am, pleasure to ride with you. I've heard good things." Brody's hand claimed hers and didn't let go. "Don't mind me saying, ma'am, you are a might pretty woman too."

Justin fisted one hand. Brody's Texan charm nauseated him.

"No, Mr. Carmichael, I don't mind at all. You're an attractive man yourself." She inclined her head, giving Brody a flirty smile.

"If we're done with the pleasantries, can we get to work?" Justin cut in, his voice rough.

~

"Move around her, Brody. Pressure her. Don't just draft off her," Justin bellowed into the Com.

"Well, now, Kid, I would do that if I could even catch her." Brody's frustrated snarl sounded back over the Com.

"Cass, let him move around you. You can't get a feel for the competition if you don't allow him close enough. Brody's good but there are better drivers than him out there, and I guarantee you won't be in the front against them."

He heard Cass laugh over the Com as she entered the banked turn. The Tucson track was known for its compound banking turns, which radiated from six to nine to twelve degrees from the bottom to the top of the turns.

"Brody, catch me if you can."

Justin grimaced as she moved to the top of the turn, allowing Brody next to her. They were two abreast on the backstretch and Cass began pushing Brody to the apron of the track. Brody accelerated forward while she moved around the back of his car. They entered the far turn, and she whipped onto the inside, passing Brody, then moved in front again.

"Nice, Cass. Keep it steady, hold your line, stay in the groove," Justin said, impressed by her ability to move around the track with expertise and control.

"Brody, defy her. You're a NASCAR driver, one of the best. Are you going to let a woman beat you?"

Smiling at Brody's rumbling reply, Justin watched him move back and forth, attempting to pass. Cass bested him every time, cruising faultlessly over the track.

The two fuchsia Grand Prix cars raced by Justin, jockeying for position. He sat back.

Now we have a race.

Brody crept up onto Cass' rear, nudging her. She jerked at her steering wheel. The car followed her move, as it was built to do. Justin stood.

"Easy, Cass," he warned, "get a feel for it. It won't be the last time."

"Keep it up, Brody, let her feel what it's like," he ordered.

Brody nudged her again and Justin heard her swear.

"Not very ladylike," Justin commented. "Cass, travel back and forth and shake him off or get out of the way."

He heard her go, "Hmph," and watched her move back and forth. Brody continued to try to slip around her, bumping her on both sides. She countered each of his moves, not allowing him the luxury of passing.

Lee and the remainder of the team littered the pit area with him as they admired the two drivers. Lee was on the Com playing the role of spotter, the person positioned high in the grandstands, in radio contact with the driver and the crew chief. The spotters alerted the drivers to any on-track obstructions, accidents or debris during the race and informed the crew when the driver is entering pit road for service. Today Lee was simply calling out times on each lap and giving them remaining laps.

Justin wasn't as relaxed as the others. He watched Cass at every turn as Brody pressured her from behind. Anything could happen.

Cass was hot, tired, and her concentration was waning. Glancing in her one rear view mirror, she rapidly scanned from Brody to the track.

Suddenly he passed her and she swore. Her fatigue was getting to her. After four hours of a non-stop driving battle with Brody in the stifling heat, she was bone weary. She moved back and forth, trying to pass him and return to her previous position. Into her ear came that annoying voice.

"Get it back, Cass."

Frustrated, she retorted, "I know what I need to do, Kid, for Christsakes."

"Okay, guys, let's call it a day, bring in the cars."

"No, don't, Justin, have some confidence in me," she demanded.

"I say it's time to pack it in."

"I say it's not," she shouted into the microphone.

"Okay," Justin said.

Concentrating on trying to work through her fatigue, she moved up on Brody. She bumped into his rear several times, her steering wheel jerking painfully against her hands.

They approached the front stretch. She moved behind him right, then left several times, trying to throw him off balance so by the time they went into the far turn he wouldn't know which way she was going to move. She zipped to the inside of the track on the curve and he moved with her, effectively blocking her. She eased high, closing in on the wall; she heard the voice of reason in her ear.

"Not smart, get away from the wall. You shouldn't be going high on that curve. You could break away from the track."

She ignored Justin and continued to ride the wall with Brody blocking her. Coming off the wall, she stayed directly behind him, riding his bumper until they entered the gradient curve. She hugged the wall again, Brody directly in front of her.

"Cass, I don't know what you're trying to do, but get off the wall!" Justin's voice snapped like a whip.

There, she instinctively saw her move. Jerking her hands with lighting speed, she used the G-force at the end of the turn to help catapult her. Then she pulled down to the bottom of the curve, stomped on the accelerator and passed him. She screamed in excitement, hearing Brody curse. They flew across the front stretch, Cass ahead of Brody.

"Pull it in, both of you. Now." Justin's command left no room for argument.

Cass and Brody pulled into the pit area. Cass removed her gloves and remained in the car, leaning her head against the steering wheel. She knew she was in for a tongue-lashing.

She saw Justin stride toward the car. She pulled her helmet off. He leaned in the window, tension lines around his mouth, a muscle in his cheek pulsing.

"When I tell you not to do something, you better damn well listen to me."

Cass sighed while Justin helped her remove her harness and extracted her bodily from the car. Her head drooping, she leaned against the car. Brody approached them. She waved him away with her hand and he made a 180-degree turn and headed in the exact opposite direction. Her head still bent forward like a wilting flower, she waited for Justin to finish.

"I am here to save your ass," he yelled. "I'm not talking to you to hear the sound of my own voice."

Watching him, she decided she was in for a long lecture. She slid down the car, plopping onto the ground. She started to undo the top of her racing suit, pulling off the fire protector from her head.

"Are you listening to me? Are you hearing what I am telling you?" he shouted.

She glared at him. "I'm not sure how I couldn't with you yelling."

"I am not yelling." His voice lowered but now it shook with his anger.

Cass sighed and rested her head back against the car. Maybe if she took a little rest, he wouldn't notice. She thought she heard him yelling again and she tried to tune him out.

Justin crouched down, his eyes surveying her exhausted face.

"Here." He handed her a water bottle.

Cass opened her eyes and took the water, drinking it, and pouring some over her head. It gave little relief from the 105-degree smoldering heat. When she looked at the track it was as if she was seeing a mirage, the heat radiating like an overheated oven off the paved oval track.

"Cass, you're too reckless sometimes. You need to rein in. The wall is a dangerous line to take on that turn."

"No."

"What?"

She looked at him. She was determined to make her point. "No, Justin, there is nothing wrong with the way I drive. The only one who needs to let go is you. You have to trust me. I know what I'm doing. It's you who concerns me. For some reason you don't want me to do what you know I'm capable of. I think it's you who's scared. Maybe you need to examine that."

A pained expression graced Justin's face and he stood. He gave her one last look, threw up his hands, then turned and walked away. "See you later," he called out.

Cass was hurt by his rejection and his unwillingness to discuss her reservations. "Don't count on it," she yelled back at him.

She saw him pause, and he continued to walk. Brody came over, as if he'd waited for Justin to leave. He sank down next to her, and she noticed his exhaustion mirrored hers.

They were training long hours to prepare Cass for her first Nextel Cup race. If they trained more hours than was necessary in this extreme heat, on this difficult track, then maybe, just maybe, she would have a better chance of surviving her first race in February against the best in the business. But the heat and the long hours in the car were killing them. Despite having Gatorade in the car, they were sweating more than they could take in.

"I sense a healthy amount of tension between you and your trainer." Brody took a sip of the water she offered him.

They sat close and relief washed over her. When Brody touched her, she felt a kinship like that of a sibling. She didn't feel the burn of desire she felt with Justin. She'd begun to think maybe she was a wanton, sex-starved woman and she would feel the same way with any man. But sitting next to this good-looking man confirmed her feelings for Justin weren't because he was hotter than today's weather. They were special.

Then her relief was replaced by a stronger feeling of alarm. What did she feel toward Justin, a man not only wounded in his body but in his soul too?

"It's the elements, the heat. It will be fine, don't worry," she finally answered Brody. She retrieved the water and they drank in companionship.

"I'm not worried. You're one hell of a driver. I hope Justin doesn't hold you back or make you doubt yourself."

Cass turned to him and gave him the kind of smile she might give a brother. "We are going to be good friends, aren't we?"

Brody returned her smile with one that could charm a salesman. Even though she wasn't attracted to him, she admired his wavy, sandy blond short hair and big blue eyes. Combined with his terrific body, he was overall a nice package.

Brody touched his race hat. "Yes, ma'am, I think we are." He put his arm around her shoulder.

"But that's all we are going to be, friends, aren't we?" She heard him sigh, as if in relief that he didn't have to pretend to charm her any more.

"I think I would like that, friends." He held out his other hand to hers and they shook with silent agreement. He hauled his lean body up, and locking his hand around her arm, he pulled her off the ground.

"Let's get out of this heat before we puddle," he said, "and make a run to the bathroom before we bust."

She laughed and looped her arm around his shoulder companionably. They made their respective bathroom stops and met up again.

"I think I need to take a cool bath." She followed him to the parking lot.

He nodded. "I'll drop you off. I'm at the hotel next to the raceway."

"Why?" she asked, turning to stop their progress. His eyes followed something in the parking lot and her gaze mimicked his. Justin had pulled up in the Jeep and was staring at them with intense dislike. Unsure why, Cass dropped her arm from around Brody's shoulder.

Brody lowered his voice. "I guess Lee was worried how the Kid would react to the competition." He touched her arm and nodded toward Justin.

Cass looked from Brody to Justin. If it was possible, Justin's stony face had taken an even deeper furious look.

"Get in," Justin snapped. "I'll take you home."

Cass turned toward Brody and he gave her an *I told you so* expression.

"That's okay, Brody will take me."

"I wasn't asking. Get in. Carmichael, see you tomorrow 6:00 a.m."

Brody looked relieved. He nodded and backed off. "See you tomorrow," he said to Cass, and headed off.

"That was rude," Cass said, then fumbled with her seat belt as Justin roared out of the track parking lot.

"Justin," she cried out, jerking against the seat as he recklessly pulled out of the track entrance.

He ignored her remark. "I forbid you to become involved with Brody. He's part of your training team, not your lover," he snarled, expertly negotiating a sharp turn.

"Stop the jeep," Cass ordered.

"What, are you crazy?" He kept driving.

"I said stop the jeep. Now."

He gave her a fuming glance. Cass held onto the dash as he swerved over to a wide spot in the road. Very deliberately, she removed her seatbelt and opened the small Jeep door. She hopped down to the ground and began walking. She heard Justin jump out and run after her.

"What are you doing? It's 105 degrees out here. You'll die of heatstroke before you reach the ranch."

She shrugged and kept walking, her racing boots crunching against the road. A hand like a vise around her upper arm wrenched her around.

"Cass…"

She stopped his words with the ones she had been so angrily holding in. "Listen, you don't tell me who I have relationships with, you don't tell me how to ride my motorcycle, and I'm even doubting you can tell me how to drive."

By the look of pain flicking across his face, her last remark hit a nerve and went right down to the bone. She felt instant remorse and put her hand on his arm.

"I'm sorry. You make me so damn angry, I don't know what I say sometimes. Why do you feel this need to always have conflict between us?" she asked as her hand reluctantly left his arm.

"You're right. I don't think I have what it takes to make you a good driver." He turned and walked to the edge of the road, staring out at the Arizona landscape.

Cass moved next to him and curved her hand on his shoulder. "Why?" she asked.

As if striking out at her comfort, he shucked her hand off his shoulder, grabbed it and pulled it to the scar running from the corner of his eye down of the side of his face. "Because of this," he yelled, his voice tormented. He pulled her hand to his arm, pressing her fingers against the scar there. "And this, and all the other scars that are there." He was panting as if the revelation had cost him more that he was willing to admit.

"Strike me," he ordered, pulling her hand against the scar on his face again.

She yanked her hand free. "No."

He reached out, clasped her hand and pulled it against his face. "Hit me, I'll block it, just do it."

The anguish in his eyes made her obey him. She brought up her open hand and sent it toward the side of his face. At the last minute his hand came up but completely missed hers, and her hand lightly slapped the side of his face. She gasped and immediately placed her fingers on his cheek.

"I'm sorry!" she cried.

He sighed and removed her hand, keeping it locked in his. "I couldn't even see it coming. The doctors say it's a depth perception problem with my peripheral vision created by the blow to the side of my head. I'm lucky I even have this eye, lucky I can see enough when I look straight forward to drive a vehicle, and that is very limited."

Swallowing, his hand squeezed hers. "Don't you see, Cass? Maybe you're right, maybe I'm projecting my problems on to you. I haven't even stepped onto a track since the accident, and all I smell when I'm out there is my own fear, my own memories, when I see you drive amazingly like I did before the accident."

"Justin, tell me what happened. The accident…?" she asked gently. She lifted her arm and stroked his cheek.

He was silent, pulling away. He began surveying the rocky sierra colored plains again. Finally he shrugged.

"There's not much to tell. It was the last race in the series. Another driver and I were close on points, so close that the placement of the last race determined the outcome of the Series winner. I was under tremendous pressure from my sponsors. I was running in first place most of the race, and on the last lap I became reckless. The driver behind me was pushing me at every turn. Going into the third turn he did a rear bump, taking off my bumper, then pushed my side.

"We were close to the wall, I was running top first into the turn. I panicked and began scraping the wall. My tire blew and I hit the wall full force. All I remember after that is a sick nauseating feeling like I had gone too many rounds on the merry-go-round at the fair. The next thing I knew I was in the hospital and my career was over, doctors telling me I was lucky to escape with my life."

He turned and made eye contact with her, as if he was daring her to pity him. "I swore when I was lying in the hospital bed and in the year it took me to recover that I would never set foot on a track again." He laughed in a cynical way. "Don't you see, you were right? It isn't your skills I'm worried about, because every time I see you on that track I see myself and I see that hospital. And each time you run next to that concrete wall, I get that sick feeling in my stomach. It makes me want to run back to the ranch and never leave."

He clenched her shoulders. "I'm no good for you. I'll hinder you, not help you. I think we should find you another trainer." He released her shoulders and took two steps back.

Fury swept through Cass. How dare he give up on her so easily? So that's what he had been doing at the ranch—hiding. She closed the distance and lightly slapped him on the cheek again. He tried to block her, his hand once more missing hers.

"You're a coward, Justin Steed," she said.

She heard his growl of outrage. She lifted her hand again to slap him. This time he caught her hand and roughly pulled it against his chest.

"Thought you couldn't do that," she said, victory ringing in her voice.

He looked at her with a shocked expression.

"Surprised yourself, didn't you?" She smiled at him and the pressure on her hand lightened.

"I saw it coming." He tried to make excuses but his voice was not convincing.

"And you'll see it coming again. I won't let you give up on this. You have so much valuable information to share. Together we can win this Series and make this happen."

Her eyes sought his, trying to read his expression. He still held her hand against his chest but his grip loosened.

"And you will lay off this angry boy routine," she continued, "and become the partner you vowed to be the first day we met, and this animosity between us will cease."

The corner of his mouth quirked. He moved closer, shaking his head. She smelled his familiar sexy male scent, now mixed with perspiration, the scent that clicked on that desire switch in her body. They both sweated as they stood in the smoldering heat, but she was starting to feel even hotter on the inside.

God, what this man does to me should be illegal.

She watched a drop run down his forehead to his cheek over his jaw, then disappear into the top of his shirt. In a way she wished she *were* that drop of water, exploring the same path. She swallowed as his mouth moved closer to hers. He was so close she could feel the breath puffing from his lips.

"Why are you shaking your head?" she said, her voice cracking. "We can't continue like this."

He shook his head again, almost as if he was in a trance. He was staring at her lips. In a low voice, he said, "Cassandra." Her name came as a caress from his lips. It was the first time he had used her given name and it made her feel feminine.

"That anger and animosity is the only thing that keeps me…" He stopped as his hands roamed down her back. Pausing at her ass, he pressed her against his erection.

With a throaty whisper, she murmured, "Keeps you from what?"

A growl emitted from his throat, his gentleness gone. Hands on her ass, he lifted her up, pulling her legs around his body and bringing her wet pussy grinding against his arousal.

It was her turn to groan. His lips hovered over hers, as if he was attempting to restrain himself but was losing the battle.

"From doing this," he said, his voice husky.

She sighed in satisfaction when his lips finally claimed hers. It was not a gentle kiss and Cass was glad. It was a hard, possessive kiss, his lips slanting over hers, his tongue playing with hers, his hands holding her as if he never wanted to let her go. He deepened the invasion, his tongue crossing with hers, dominating her.

Cass reveled in his roughness, knowing he wasn't going to be a gentle lover. He drew her body up harder against his, jockeying her for a stronger position, pushing her further into him. She moaned in response.

Suddenly a car of kids drove by and honked their horn, hooting and laughing. Justin jerked back and dropped her legs back to the ground. He stepped away from her, as if he were caught by his parents making love to his high school sweetheart in the back of his car.

They were both out of breath, glistening with sweat. Whether it was from the heat or their passionate kiss, Cass didn't know. He grabbed her arm and they stumbled back to the Jeep. He pushed her into the passenger side and he went around to the driver's.

Sliding in, he watched as she splashed water on her face and upper body. Aware of his gaze, she handed him the water bottle and he poured it over his head. She watched his shirt stick to his body and shifted in her seat.

"The anger and hurtful words between us will end. I don't care what the repercussions are. Matter of a fact," she wiped her hands on her shirt, and saw Justin's eyes following her movements, "I kind of like them."

She smiled at him then and Justin slowly smiled back, so brilliantly she drew in her breath. She wondered if revealing his supposed flaws to her had released his fears, like a cage door opening and his doubts winging away.

"Whatever the repercussions? Are you sure about that?" A flame burned in his eyes, and she felt an answering burn inside her.

"Definitely, very sure. Whatever the consequences. Are we partners now, one hundred percent loyalty, no going back partners?"

He laughed, and Cass stared in amazement. He seemed younger, as if confiding his fears had taken years off of him. Still grinning, he removed the emergency brake and put the car into gear.

"There are only two, no, maybe three, things I am sure of, Cassandra."

She shivered, delighted at the way her name flowed off his tongue. "Uh huh, what are they?"

"Death," he said immediately.

She gave him a cross look.

"Taxes."

"And the third?" For some reason, she held her breath.

"You." He released the clutch and surged onto the road.

Cass smiled as he took them home. She had won the first round but there were more rounds to come, and she planned to win those too.

After all, I'm a competitor. But so is he.

Chapter Seven

Their relationship changed after that. Gone were the anger and sarcastic remarks and in their place was an attractive, possessive, hard working, relentless trainer who Cass thanked God every day for being on her side. Her focus was winning—that was all she could afford to think about.

They hadn't talked again about her relationship with Brody, although there were times when she and Brody had their heads stuck together going over her race strategy and she sensed Justin's irritation. If she didn't know any better, she would say that he was jealous, even though it was clear she and Brody were only good friends.

They trained the rest of the week without incident. She felt a strong connection develop between her and Justin. There were times when she knew what he was going to say before his voice came squawking in her helmet or what he was thinking before he told it to her.

He hadn't touched her since the incident on the road. He kept their relationship on a strictly business level, most of the time avoiding her when they were away from the track, seemingly engaged in the business of the ranch. Cass was starting to think the incident had never happened. Maybe it was a figment of her imagination, a fantasy she tried to bring to life.

They were finishing up training the next Thursday evening when Justin approached her.

"There's a race here Saturday. If you want to test your skills, I think we can get a volunteer crew and a car to enter into the Sportsman Late Model division. It's a small race, but it will get you a little experience with a larger field before we hit the big time."

She nodded while she stripped off her gear. Unzipping her bright fuchsia race uniform, she noticed Justin's eyes following her actions, his eyes taking on a smoky desiring look as she peeled down to her sports bra. A smile formed on her lips. So he wasn't as immune as she'd thought.

~

In Saturday's qualifying, Cass ran with the best time, putting her in first pole position at the start of the final race later that evening. Justin and Brody were there, along with a few volunteer crew members. Surprisingly, Justin had found two cars, one for her and one for Brody. Brody had taken second position behind Cass and they were racing as a team. The Sportsman Modified was a little different than a NASCAR Nextel stock car, but the basic concepts of driving never changed.

Cass and Brody lounged in pit row waiting for the pre-post meeting. Justin approached them, a clipboard in his hand. He was recording stats tonight because Lee had the night off.

He was handsome as ever in his Lovely Cosmetics racing jersey and cap. His hair was getting longer, poking out around the back of his cap. He had his sunglasses on, as usual, and shorts. His slightly broken stride as he strode toward them didn't detract from the man as a whole. He was fantastic, and Cass found herself extremely distracted when he was around.

She had tried to approach him several times since his roadside confession, but he usually found reasons to evade any lengthy conversation with her, almost as if he was avoiding her. Cass was convinced more than ever that she needed to sleep with him. That maybe if she experienced sex with him, her distracting thoughts would vanish, allowing her to focus on her driving.

She laid her hand on Brody's shoulder. Maybe it wasn't Justin she needed. Maybe any man would do. Maybe she just needed sex. Brody was as good as any—better, in fact, than most—and she knew it wouldn't take much to seduce him. Out of the corner of her eye, she watched him turn his head to look at her. Although she spoke to him, she kept her gaze on Justin.

"You and I are going to celebrate a tough week after this race today, Brody," she said. "The two of us. I have a little favor to ask you, something I'd like you to take care of for me."

She finally turned and gave him her most engaging smile. He smiled back in his charming, good-looking way. Her heart still didn't skip a beat. He placed a hand over the top of hers on his shoulder.

"You bet, anything for my girl." He patted her hand as if she was a child.

She laughed. *If he only knew.*

Justin's eyes narrowed when he saw Cass touch Brody. When she did that there was a primitive reaction in Justin that wanted to tear Brody apart piece by piece. That same primal part of his brain wanted to claim Cass for his own, to declare she was his exclusively.

He heard her tell Brody they were going to celebrate tonight, and by her mischievous smile he knew she was up to something. He glared at her, shaking his head. She lifted her chin in response and flipped back her hair, showing him how seriously she took his threats.

His mouth tightened in anger. She was messing with fire again.

"You two ready?" he asked, watching them rise and grab their gear. "Go ahead, Brody. I want a word with Cass."

Cass nodded at Brody. Acknowledging her okay, he tugged the rim of his cap and left them alone.

"What are you up to?" Justin demanded.

"Why do you ask?"

"Don't look at me like that. I know you, and I can tell."

Her eyes went from innocent to stormy. "I think I already told you I don't need a mother." She grabbed her gear and started to leave. He reached out and placed his hand on her arm to stop her.

"I think we both know you have some sort of devious plan in mind."

Shaking off his hand, she smiled at him. He looked at her, suspicions filling him.

"I'm going out with Brody tonight. Actually, I was going to ask you, but you don't seem in the mood lately." Her secret smile made uneasiness twirl inside his gut.

"What the hell are you talking about?" he asked, his voice rising.

"Nothing." She ran her finger hand down his jaw and murmured, "Too bad." Then she walked off, her hips swinging.

His heart continued to beat rapidly as it always did when she touched him. She had the ability to stir him any place, any time. That's why he'd been avoiding her outside the track lately. He was afraid he would lose his control and go much further than a kiss. Even her scent when she stood near him left him wanting. Watching her strut away, he worried. He could smell trouble brewing, and she was the cause.

~

Cass won the race. She and Brody blew away the field, running neck in neck until Cassandra stopped playing with him. Despite Brody's above average driving abilities, it was clear Cass outshined him three times over.

Both were jovial when they had finished receiving their awards and pulled into the pit directly outside of the track. Justin watched Cass closely. It had gotten dark and was around 10:00 p.m.

Approaching Justin, she called over her shoulder to Brody. "Meet you there. I need to shower."

She was smiling when she neared Justin.

He nodded at her. "Nice driving tonight."

"I need the Jeep, Dad," she drawled, as if rubbing his face in his newly declared role.

He pulled the keys out of his pocket. Fighting the desire to keep his fist closed, he opened his fingers and handed them to her.

"Can you get a ride home?" she asked before taking them.

"Yeah, I'm going to help the boys. One of them will drop me off at home. What's up?"

She threw her gear into the car. "Going out. Don't expect me home anytime early tonight. Did Lee fly home for the weekend?"

Nodding, Justin gritted his teeth. Something wasn't quite right. He wanted to interrogate her so bad he could taste it, but he knew she would resist and clam up even more. He tried to act casual.

"So where's the party tonight?" He followed her as she walked out to the parking lot.

"Oh," she waved her hand vaguely, jumping into the Jeep, "meeting some friends at Marty's." She named the local bar.

"Friends, huh. Brody too?" Although he tried to sound casual, he felt his anger bubbling up.

"That's the plan." Her voice was clipped as she strapped on her seat belt.

"Cass," he said, his voice harsh with warning.

"We've had this discussion. Let's not rehash it, okay? See you later. Have a good night." She waved at him, cutting off any further discussion.

He watched her thoughtfully. Maybe he would do a little partying of his own tonight in the local bar. The corners of his mouth curved up. That would put a little damper on her fun, wouldn't it?

~

Justin's eyes began to water, his body becoming pleasantly numb from his third scotch on the rocks. For the last hour he had sat at the barstool, drinking, sucking in secondhand smoke and working himself into a rage as he eyed Brody and Cass.

Cass was dressed to kill and that's what it appeared she was trying to do. Justin growled as he stared at the dance floor. Cass was literally wrapped around Brody, glued closer than there should have been a legal right to be. Her simple black dress clung to her in all the right places. His gaze devoured her form, the bareness of her shoulders and arms to the rise of her breasts, to the slenderness of her waist and over the curves of her hips, dropping down to rest on her shapely ankles.

Justin watched as her body swayed to the music of *Lady* while she pressed against Brody. One slender hand held a drink she occasionally sipped, the other circled around Brody's neck.

Brody was continually shaking his head at her, as if he was denying a repeated request. But as the night wore on, Justin noticed Brody's head was shaking less and less.

Justin's drink was poised when Cass lifted her hands and flattened her palms on the sides of Brody's head. The glass froze a quarter inch from Justin's mouth. He blinked his eyes to make sure he was still seeing straight. He slammed his drink onto the bar, seeing Cass pull Brody's head down to hers.

At first Brody seemed to be resisting her, then his arms slowly started to encircle her, so slow it was almost reluctant. Justin watched as Brody tightened his hold on her.

All right, that was *enough*. Justin surged out of his chair. Steadying himself, he started off in Cass' direction. He pushed between dancing couples, ignoring their glares, until he reached the unsuspecting couple. His arm whipped out and he hauled Brody out of Cass' arms.

At first Brody seemed stunned, as if someone had hit him on the head. Then the Cass-induced haze left his eyes. Justin heard him swear and it became easier to pull him back. Justin watched Cass' half-lidded perusal of him as she smiled.

"Justin, nice of you to join us." She flipped her hand in the direction of her table. "Would you like a drink?" As if taking his silence as an affirmative, she sauntered over to their table and eased down onto a chair.

Justin grabbed one of the spare chairs, turning it around and straddling it. He was surprisingly alert considering the amount of booze he had consumed on an empty stomach. He placed his hand along the top of the chair, laid his chin on his arms and let his gaze worship Cass.

She had piled her hair on top of her head in a mound of blonde fullness. Small curls escaped her attempt at confinement and drifted around her face, giving her a soft feminine look. Feminine, hell … this was all woman. He wanted to own her.

Cass watched, half-lidded, while Justin's eyes fixed on her. She could see his desire and she liked it. All night she had been trying to convince Brody to sleep with her, hoping if she scratched that itch her body would give up on Justin. Being the gentleman that he was and the friend he claimed to be, Brody continued to deny her. She knew Justin had been lurking at the bar. She had seen him, but chose to ignore him and her attraction.

She was reaching a chink in Brody's armor when the man who'd been on her mind all night appeared. He looked fantastic. His short-sleeved western shirt accented his broad shoulders and muscular arms. His black jeans hugged his hard body. His black cowboy boots finished off the outfit.

Does anything faze this man?

He even smelled wonderful. His spicy masculine cologne drifted over her, making her close her eyes momentarily with desire. Although she had been trying so hard to forget herself tonight, every time Brody had touched her or looked at her, she saw Justin. A few minutes ago, she imagined she was locking her body and her lips against Justin instead of Brody.

She opened her eyes. They strayed first to Justin, then to Brody. She saw guilt and even regret in Brody's face. He smiled and reached across to tap her hand.

"I've got to go, Cass." He got up and walked around the back, bending to whisper in her ear, "Before I do something we'll both regret."

She shivered at his words as he dropped a light kiss onto her neck. He was right. She'd been a fool to think he could replace what she really craved.

I am an idiot to ignore Justin.

Brody slapped Justin on the back as he moved toward the door. "Can I trust you to get her safely home, my friend?" He gave Justin a fierce look.

Justin nodded and held out his hand, waiting for Cass to give him the keys. After she dropped them in his palm, Brody said he would enjoy the short walk back to the hotel and he left.

Cass sighed and turned back to Justin. "It looks like you've been elected by default."

He frowned, as if suspicious of her meaning. She gave him what she hoped was a sensual grin. Rising, she pulled his hand and swung him onto the dance floor. Embracing him, she pressed her body against his.

For a minute he forgot her words while he inhaled her scent and relished in the feel of her body hugged against his. Then he remembered her words. "Elected for what?" he asked.

"To satisfy my lust, of course." She placed her hand against his beating heart.

"What?" He skidded to a halt and placed both of his hands on her bare shoulders, shaking her. "Did I hear you right?" At that moment, he questioned his sanity. Was he hearing what he wanted to hear or what she really said?

She sighed. Reaching up, she pulled Justin's arms around her body, settling his hands on her ass.

"It's distracting me, you're distracting me. Something I can't afford. I've decided I need to scratch this itch. I preferred you but Brody was going to have to do in a pinch. Outside of the track you don't seem very interested in conversing with me, so I was improvising with Brody."

She pulled in closer, rubbing her body against his, putting his senses on full alert. On this sultry evening, with this beautiful woman, her scent, her body, his inebriation, he was having a difficult time forgetting his reluctance.

"Unfortunately, he was becoming difficult to convince, so now that he's gone the job falls to you."

"You're drunk." He stated the obvious as if he was trying to find a reason behind her craziness.

She tilted her head to the side, considering his statement. Nodding, she turned back to the task at hand.

"Undoubtedly." Sliding closer, she slowly, erotically ran her hand over his chest along his shirt collar until she came in contact with the skin exposed in the vee of his shirt. Her hand slipped inside his collar around the back of his neck and into his hair. He moaned and bent his head closer to her lips. Her eyes were at half-mast now, smoldering hard and fast with desire.

"Let me get this straight," he breathed against her lips. "You want me to satisfy your lust." His lips were barely touching hers. His tongue came out to lightly trail her lips, licking off the taste of Brody. He did it on purpose. She needed to understand it was him she was with, not some second-hand man.

"Tonight you want to sleep with me." He continued to say the words like a chant. His lips were burning into hers now, not waiting for her answer. He swayed her body against his and slowly devoured her lips.

"I'm not a gentle lover, Cass. I'm not sure I'm your best choice." He raised his head from hers to stare deeply into her eyes, giving her a chance to say no. It must be the alcohol, he thought, because he couldn't think of a reason not to grant her demand.

"Justin," she drew his cheek against hers and whispered against his ear in a lover's caress. "I'm as sure as I am when I get into the cockpit of that NASCAR that we will make wild, mad, passionate love. I think I've always been sure, since the first minute we met."

Her words sent his desire soaring. He hugged her hard against him. Then he pulled back and grabbed her hand. "Come on, let's get out of here."

~

The ride to the ranch only took minutes. They hurried into the house, but instead of heading to the bedroom Justin steered her toward the back of the house. He pulled out his keys and unlocked a room he'd never shown to her before.

He heard Cass pull in a breath. It was an inside jungle, a paradise. Tropical plants lined the room like pillars, surrounding a small Jacuzzi with a waterfall. Around the side of the Jacuzzi was a small workout area. The floors were littered with a dozen chaise lounges. Justin leaned against the door and watched the joy on her classically lined face. This was the room where he escaped from all the pressure.

"It's beautiful," she breathed. Stopping in the middle of the floor she sank onto a chaise. The slit in her skirt shimmied up almost to the side of her ass. Justin pushed off from the door jamb and strode toward her.

He felt sober, sure he wanted to make love to this woman in this place and this time. He wanted it more than he had ever wanted anything in his life. He slowly descended to his knees, facing her. Her hands came up to rest on his chest. He watched as she began to unbutton his shirt. He wanted and he was going to take. He resigned himself to his fate.

She stopped and looked into his eyes. "Tell me what you want, what pleases you," she said, her voice a throaty whisper.

She watched as he placed his hands on hers and very gently pushed her hands away. Then he grabbed the two sides of his shirt and ripped it apart. Buttons went flying and for the first time his full naked chest was revealed to her. She gasped, staring at it. With the exception of a scar close to his ribs he was a perfectly formed male.

"Touch me," he said roughly. He leaned his head down and sipped from her lips.

She ran her hands the length of his chest over his nipples up to his broad, muscular shoulders. She shucked the rest of his shirt off while he dropped his arms to let it fall.

"God, you are beautiful," she said. Reaching forward she placed a passionate kiss on his chest. She felt his breath suck in. She loved the taste of him, the texture of his skin against her lips. As long as she lived, she wasn't sure she would ever enjoy a man the way she planned to do Justin.

"Are you sure about this?" he said with a moan.

For an answer, she ran her tongue over his nipples, lapping at each one. "I'm sure." She chuckled against his chest when he growled.

He forced her head from his chest and dragged her lips against his, angling his head so he could deepen the kiss. Her hands climbed up his chest to wrap around his shoulders. He broke off the kiss, leaning back.

"Are you protected? We're not teenagers, we don't need any accidents."

She nodded affirmatively as she ran her thumb lightly over his lips.

"If you're not sure," he continued, "say stop at any time, promise me?" He framed her face with his hands, forcing her eyes to meet his.

She nodded again. Staring at him, she slid closer to his lips. His eyes drifted slowly closed as she pressed her lips tentatively to his. She ran her hands down his chest and stopped when his jeans blocked further exploration. He broke off from her lips and ran kisses down her jaw to her neck and shoulder. Cass leaned back her head to give him better access. Eyes closed, she absorbed the sensation of his cool lips on her hot skin. His smell was driving her crazy.

His touch is incredible.

She felt his hand move. Through her sensual haze, she became aware of cooler air invading her skin. His hands touched her bare back as he lowered her zipper, lower and lower until it touched the small of her back. She wore nothing underneath the dress and she felt his excitement mounting. He slowly drew the dress over her shoulders and let it pool at her waist. She felt the silk slide against her naked skin. A reminder that there would be nothing left between them when it slipped to the floor.

"Cass," he murmured, his voice husky. His hands reached out and eased down her shoulders, inching farther, lower to her front. When he cupped her breasts in his hands, Cass' breath caught. His thumbs and forefinger lightly skimmed her nipples, gently pinching them, causing them to harden. The sensation gave her more pleasure than she had ever imagined. Tension stirred in her stomach, and the heat radiated lower to her pussy, causing a rush of pulsating moisture. Need followed the rush.

She moaned, allowing her head to fall back, arching in pleasure. His rough callused hands skimmed around to her back and his mouth took the place of his fingers.

Cass cried out. Her head coming forward, she watched him lean over her, lapping each breast, his tongue tasting each nipple. There was something so erotic about watching him. Her fingers delved into his hair as the pressure of his hands on her back increased and eased her breasts closer into his mouth. He sucked, licked and tasted each breast as if it was a hard candy to be savored. She felt like a volcano awaiting eruption.

"Ahhhh, Justin," she groaned, her voice fevered. "I need … I need…"

He lifted his head, then his lips returned to hers. "Tell me, babe, tell me what you need."

"I need to touch all of you."

He leaned up and pulled her to a standing position. His hands made a full sweep of her body, completely tugging off her dress.

She stepped out of it.

She was naked from head to toe as he slid her body against his. He ran his large, rough hands from her hair down her back, cupping her ass with his hands. Her fingers strayed to the top of his jeans. She wanted them off.

"God, you are breathtaking." He ran his tongue down her neck. She tugged at his jeans, fumbling with his buckle. He reached down and pulled off his boots and socks, then his hands curved over hers and together, hands lightly touching, they rid him of his jeans.

Cass pushed at his briefs, his arousal evident, his penis seeking relief from its confinement. Bending, she skimmed his briefs down his legs as he stepped out of them. She stayed where she was, her hands still touching his legs.

She was amazed by the power she saw.

His cock was full, veined, and pulsing; standing proud, nestled in black fur. It was the hugest penis she had ever seen, long and wide. She was surprised, not sure if they would fit. She raised her hand tentatively. She wanted to feel it so bad, wanted to taste him. His hand rested lightly on her head.

"Explore as much as you want."

She did just that. Reaching out a hand, she touched his arousal. It bucked against her hand.

"It wants you, babe." He chuckled.

Becoming bolder, Cass wrapped her entire hand around him, stroking him. It was rough yet smooth, like the finest velvet. She ran her hand up and down. She noticed he stopped chuckling and was making small grunting noises. She stroked him harder. He thrust into her hands. She had strong hands and she wasn't afraid to use them. His enjoyment told her to continue.

"God, Cass." His knees gave way. Pulling himself from her hands, he sank down onto the cushion with her. His hands delved into her hair, spraying pins everywhere as he released it from its confinement. With both hands on her head, he brought her lips to his, devouring, burrowing with his tongue, mating with her mouth. He reached down and roughly pulled her legs around him while he lowered her to the cushion.

Her legs automatically spread as he pressed into her, and he gently probed her with his dick. Wetness greeted him and she arched against his teasing.

Cass wanted him inside her in the worst way. She hurt with longing.

He drew away and she cried out in loss. But he came back and ran his lips and tongue down her body, tasting, kissing, and nipping her occasionally. The sensation of his mouth on her body was incredible. Cass had never experienced the craving to take that consumed her now.

Their matching breaths panted heavily. He kissed his way along her stomach to her thigh, her navel, and to the inside of her legs. His hands lightly pushed her legs farther apart, and he placed his mouth where her heat and moisture radiated from. Using fingers and tongue, he separated her labia, sucking, drinking greedily from her, sucking her clit.

"Ahhhh."

Cass cried out in pleasure, her back arched, her body jerked. Her hands of their own volition tangled in his hair, urging him on. His tongue found her most sensitive spot. With teeth and tongue, he began to rock her hips in motion to his mouth, prolonging her pleasure. Even more sensual gratification intensified her moan as he slid two fingers into her, working them back and forth. His other hand slid under her ass, tugging her into his mouth and hand. He was eating her with purpose and intent, like a hungry man with his last meal.

Give it to him.

"Ohhh, Justin, yeees! God, yeees!" Cass cried out. She couldn't help it, his hands and mouth were creating emotions of such blinding pleasure that she wanted to scream with joy. Heat radiated from her vagina where he worshiped, slithering up her body, making her skin feel as if she were on fire. She was burning up, sweet beads of water dripping off her forehead, tension building in her and begging for release.

His tongue continued to pulsate as he slid another finger into her, moving it unhurriedly up and down, gently stretching her. Suddenly arching, Cass' world exploded in hot white light. She threw her head back, and this time she did scream, wailing his name as her orgasm overtook her.

He released her. She cried out at losing the sensation, but it wasn't over. Setting both hands under her butt, he lifted her to meet him as he thrust powerfully into her.

She felt a satisfying fullness, a feeling of completeness, an oneness that was beyond reason. He froze. Cass knew there was more.

"Cassandra," he breathed her name in a caress. "Look at me."

Cass opened her eyes. He leaned over her, his mouth closing on hers, his expression so fierce and intimate it was nearly as erotic as the thickness of him inside her.

"You are mine now. Don't ever doubt it. You are mine."

She shivered, realizing he was claiming her. It was a simple statement but such a possessive, passionate one.

"Say it," he demanded.

Cass glanced into his fever-filled eyes and for a quick second she wanted to deny him. She didn't say anything, only matched his gaze. He instantly pulled back as if he would withdraw.

"No!" She wrapped her legs around his rock-hard ass to keep him from retreating.

"Say it," he demanded again.

She sighed because she knew she wasn't going to win this battle. She'd been his from the minute their hands had met.

She placed her hands on his ass and drew him back in, hard and fast. He groaned, his anxious expression hitting her right in the heart. She wrapped her hand around his neck. Bringing his mouth to hers, she kissed him gently.

"I'm yours, Justin, all the way to my toes," she vowed.

He smiled and she felt him exhale, the wind of his breath caressing her mouth. He kissed her hard then and began rocking her with age-old movements. His back arched up as he tried to fill her as much as he could, slipping in and slowly withdrawing, forward then backward, only to repeat the cycle.

He closed his eyes, and she did the same. She was lost in the sensation of his body and his rhythm. His movements continued, his tongue mingling with hers. The noises he was making could only be those of pure masculine satisfaction and pleasure. He whispered senseless words in her ears, how she was making him feel, how hard he was, how beautiful she was.

They were senseless because she was lost in her own world of bliss.

Instinctually thrusting her hips to meet his brought him deeper and more fully into her. Sex had never been like this before, ever.

She arched against him as she reached for another orgasm. Tremors shot through her, and she exclaimed wordlessly. As if he was waiting for that moment, he thrust into her one final time, as far as he could. Dropping back his head, he roared like a lion. Cass went with him.

He collapsed on top of her. His body was heavy and he remained buried inside her. She loved the feel of his body—satisfied, hard and sprawled over her own. Then he pushed up a little to allow her some room to breathe. It was a considerate gesture, a gentle one.

She knew he had a tender side, despite his claim that he didn't. He leaned down and rested a kiss on the pulse at her neck. She had her eyes closed but she still felt his closeness and his kiss. Her hands soothed over the smooth planes of his back, straying down to his ass.

Man, I am in trouble.

"Thank you," she said, hugging him to her. A part of her wanted to start bawling at the beauty of their joining. She felt a hand glide over her face and she dared to finally open her eyes.

His desire had dimmed but not completely gone, the fire still in his eyes but banked. He smiled, a sort of Cheshire Cat smile. "No. Thank you." He cupped her cheek and trailed his hand down her shoulder. She felt him stir inside of her, his penis lengthening.

She raised her eyebrows at him. He looked guilty.

Justin reared back so he wouldn't be tempted to ride her again, then reached down to raise her into his arms. She smiled at him. Unable to help himself, he kissed her, ravishing her mouth. Her enthusiastic response to his kiss almost made him forget his purpose.

Carrying her to the Jacuzzi and waterfall, he was amazed at how light she was. For such a tall woman she was so delicate.

Sometimes the thought of what might happen to her in that car drove him crazy. His arms tightened around her and she gazed at him questioningly.

Slowly he entered the warm Jacuzzi with her still in his arms. He sank into the water, setting her on his lap. She sighed against his shoulder and sank into him.

The water flowed around them, soothing him. He leaned his head back, eyes drifting closed. His hands lightly held and stroked her. All was right in his world. Too bad it was temporary. He knew what he had done was crazy. He had completely destroyed their professional relationship, but at this moment he didn't care. However temporary this was, he was going to seize it.

Cass couldn't help herself, she wanted him again, she wanted to taste him, to take in every inch of him. There was something so elemental about feeling him inside her. The pleasure of their union had been so profound for her, as if it touched a part of her soul that had never been opened before.

Leaning forward, she kissed his exposed throat. She watched him sigh in satisfaction and smile as he smoothed his hand down her back. She ran her wet hands down his neck to his chest. He continued to lean back, letting her explore him.

Cass allowed her body to float so she was straddling him while her hands strayed down lower and lower, and finally cupped his balls. His eyes opened and he began to harden.

"Has it always been so ... for you..." There were no words she could think of to describe what had happened between them.

He tangled his hands in her hair, making her look at him. He was alert now, a look in his eyes like he was approaching a tricky curve.

"Did I hurt you? I was too rough, wasn't I? I'm so big and you're so small." His eyes ran over her face, trying to read her answer in her expression.

Cass laughed, squeezing him to her. "God, no, are you kidding?" She leaned forward and whispered seductively into his ear, "The rush I got from what just happened far exceeded anything I've ever felt behind the wheel of a fast moving vehicle." It was her ultimate compliment.

"Ah," he nodded his head, "I understand. I've been behind that wheel, remember."

She laughed and kissed a spot below his ear. He moaned, his hands running down her back, then up again.

"No, it's not always this incredible." He guided her mouth to his as he nibbled on her lower lip. "Because you are an incredible woman, Cassandra, very incredible," he said between kisses. His hands moved back down again and he lifted her against his newly revived cock.

"So incredible…" She pressed herself onto him.

"Ahhh." He leaned his head back as she shifted above him. "What you do to me, it should be illegal."

His hands cradled her hips, guiding her, encouraging her to dance with him. He licked her as water and steam seeped around them, making it easy to move. He pushed her against the wall of the tub, driving into her, taking over her gentle moves with forceful ones. She felt a return of that rush she had so inadequately tried to describe.

Cass hummed with her orgasm, so quick and hot she gasped in satisfaction. Her vagina milked his dick, causing him to stiffen and spurt into her. When they had both satisfied themselves, he floated with her in his arms.

"Hmm, I thought that driving was the only thing you did well, but I can see I was wrong." He smiled against her lips, swimming them toward the waterfall. "Don't you ever forget who's the better driver of this team."

She laughed, and Justin hugged her against him.

"I won't," she said, "because there is no one who ever could compete with you."

He pulled back, his face serious. "Don't you forget." He ran his hands over her face in an attempt to soften his words.

"I won't forget it, rest assured." Her hands also came up, her thumb caressing the scar on his face. Her eyes locking with his, she saw her words had calmed the lion. He smiled at her, and she smiled back.

"I think it's time we took a shower." He moved them toward the simulated waterfall, and submerged them both despite her cries of outrage.

Chapter Eight

Six months later, February
Daytona Raceway, Daytona Beach, Florida

"How's it feel?"
"It's loose in the right rear, around the curves."
"Okay, bring it in. We'll adjust it."
Cass glanced around at the other cars, trying to find an inside line to make it into the pits. Six months of training had led her to the place she had only dreamed of being.
I'm at Daytona Raceway, Daytona Beach, Florida.
They had two weeks to practice before the Daytona 500. Like a worried father, Justin had thoroughly reviewed the track with Cass. She remembered his mini-lesson clearly. She felt every inch of the difficulty in the track. It was hard and fast with extremely high banks. Even the most experienced driver would have difficulty.
Jamming the car into third, she eased off of the track toward pit row. In her back-up car, Brody continued the run. As Cass approached her L-mark, the L-shaped line that marked

her pitting stop, the hustle of other drivers pitting around her made her cautious. All she needed to do was hit another car during practice to screw up the show.

Cass raised her face shield as Justin approached amidst a flurry of adjustment around her car. He looked edible. Even with his disheveled hair and his bright fuchsia sponsor hat resting on his head, she loved the sight of him.

In the past six months they had grown close. In between the hustle of practice they had moved from one-time lovers to all-the-time friends. Along with sharing their life stories and laughing at each other's corny jokes, Cass felt they had built a bond going beyond their everyday lives—to the track, where it was essential they use that trust implicitly.

The dream evening six months ago had not been discussed.

We have to keep a professional relationship. Our careers are on the line. I have a series to win. He has a ranch to save.

Cass continued to tell herself this, but a small part of her was unsure of Justin.

Maybe it was a one-time lay for him. Maybe he has already gotten me out of his system. Maybe I was more trouble than I was worth.

One thing was for sure. One night of passion with this man had not been enough to quench the fire that was building in her, ready to explode. She was slowly learning to deal with the distraction and to keep her focus. But it was the hardest thing she'd ever done in her life.

Justin popped his head inside the car. When she was strapped in position in the cockpit, her movement was very limited. Restricting, hot, and stressful, this was her life now.

"After this pit, you and Brody trade places drafting. I want to see how she performs."

Cass nodded, giving a thumbs up.

"After that, bring them in and we'll practice the pit, changing tires, see how we're doing."

She nodded again. Adjusting her gloves, she glanced at her gauges.

Justin stuck a water bottle into her helmet and she drank, and adjusted her safety harness. Justin pulled her helmet toward him. She glanced up, her eyes making contact with his. He had removed his headset so no one else could hear him but her. He screamed into her helmet.

"Babe, are you okay?" He had a concerned look on his face and his other hand squeezed her shoulder.

Cass smiled at his endearment. This was the first time in six months he acknowledged they had any more than a business relationship. She removed her gloves and placed her hand on his arm. He leaned farther into the car and sandwiched her hand between his. His touch transmitted a familiar warmth and calmness to her. Although she could barely hear his voice, she knew by the look in his eyes that he was worried. She shook her head, dismissing his concern. She was strong. She had to be.

At the approach of one of the pit members, he quickly released her hand. They spoke and Justin nodded. He put his headgear back on, and she heard his familiar voice in her helmet.

"You're good to go."

She replaced her gloves; Justin slammed down her visor. She gave him the final thumbs up and, jamming into first, sped out of pit row, trying to catch Brody. Easing up behind him, she heard Justin inform Brody of their plan. She inched in so close to Brody she was almost touching his bumper.

She was focused on keeping her line behind Brody.

"This is practice. Everyone should be behaving," Justin said.

"They seem to be tolerating a woman in their midst. I think you have some friends out there. Right now they don't see you as a threat. But you know on race day, all bets are off."

"Yeah, tell me about it."

Suddenly, she felt her rear jerk as another driver smashed into her.

Another car just hit me.

She spun to the right while Brody jerked to the left. She felt her tires break loose, causing her to slide. She followed the skid, her hands moving the steering wheel, while she screeched into the apron and finally came to rest at the end of the field. She did a quick assessment to see if anything was damaged. Her anger surfacing, she tried to pull herself out of the car.

"Goddamn son of a bitch." She ripped off her gloves so she could undo her harness. "What the hell was that?" she screamed into her microphone.

"Cass, calm down. Are you okay?"

"Yeah, I'm okay." Shaking with fury, she ripped off her helmet and jimmied herself out of the car. She identified the subject car from its dented fender, a black Taurus with painted teeth lined in the front and red blood dripping out them. Besides the teeth, there were endless sponsor stickers and the name "THE TERMINATOR" in white lettering across the front. She waved the car down, making its driver stop. The roar of the additional cars sped by them as he pulled off into the infield. Cass could smell the scent of burning rubber and oil. She could hear the noise of shifting gears and exhaust wafted over her, making her nostrils flare. The smell of the track was engraved into her being; like her heartbeat, it ran essential blood through her system, as important to her as breathing. Cass stomped to the driver window and started to give the driver a piece of her mind. By then Brody had pulled into the end field, and she saw Justin running across the track.

"Are you crazy to hit me like that? We're practicing, you idiot." She watched him lazily tug off his helmet. His sweat-soaked hair stuck to his head and he was smiling at her as he slowly removed his gloves, plucking off each finger with a sinister calmness Cass wasn't even close to feeling ... as if he was out for a Sunday drive. His actions infuriated her. She curled and uncurled her hands, trying to hold back from taking those gloves and shoving them down his throat.

"Wanted to meet Justin's lady," he lazily drawled.

"You wanted to ... now I *know* you're out of your mind. You could have killed me or my other driver," she screamed, knowing she was losing control and not giving a damn. Several people were running toward her. Confronting other drivers in the middle of the field didn't happen.

"Look, honey, if you can't play with the big boys ... get out of the way." He started to put back on his gloves.

"If you're such a man," Cass said, her voice chilly with disdain, "why don't you get out of that car and fight like one, instead of sitting there like a sissy."

He launched out of the car. Prepared for battle, Cass spread her legs and raised her hands.

When he struck, Cass ducked. His knuckles glanced off her cheek, but she avoided the brunt of the weight behind the blow. She stepped forward and slammed her open palms against both of his shoulders, sending him flying backward against his car. Out of the corner of her eye, she saw Justin, Brody, and a couple other men racing toward them.

"You better back off, asshole," she snapped.

He hesitated, then leapt at her. Brody jumped between them while Justin's arms came around her from behind, locking her against his chest. Another man put the same hold on her opponent. She struggled to free herself from Justin, just as the other driver fought to free himself. The more she fought to get loose, the tighter Justin's hold became. Finally, she stopped, breathing heavily. Across from her, the other guy stopped fighting too.

Justin released Cass. At the same moment, the man holding the other driver dropped his hold. His lip curled, the driver struck out, his fist catching Cass' cheek. Not expecting the attack, she fell against Justin.

Justin steadied her, then moved around her and flew at the other driver.

"You'll pay for that, McCalister." His fist smashed into the driver's chin, sending him slamming to the ground.

It was Cass' turn to hold Justin back. She jumped forward and grabbed his forearms. "No, Justin! You'll get kicked off the track."

Then hordes of red uniformed NASCAR employees swarmed around them, separating the two men. By the way Justin cradled his hand, Cass knew the punch had cost him.

Forced by the NASCAR officials to calm down, the two teams stood facing each other. Cameras and microphones were stuck in their faces.

"Mr. Steed, Mr. Steed, did you expect the rivalry between you and Beau McCalister to continue through your new driver?" a reporter shouted at Justin.

Confused, Cass frowned as she watched Justin try to compose himself.

"Now, guys, you know how high emotions get during pre-race nerves." Justin's smile looked more like a snarl, Cass thought. "Let's chalk it up to that," he continued. "My driver is a skilled professional and we look forward to facing Beau on the track this weekend. Now, if you will excuse us."

The reporters continued to shout questions as he grabbed Cass' arm and pulled her back to the car. As the NASCAR officials herded everyone back to the stands, Cass watched

Beau McCalister being hauled off toward his own car. He pointed at her and blew her a kiss.

She had a gesture she wanted to give him back, but thought of the reporters and turned to Justin instead. "Who the hell was that?" Something tickled at her cheek. She reached up to wipe it away and her hand came away red with blood.

"Shit."

Brody approached as Justin pulled a clean rag from his pocket. Holding Cass' chin, he smoothed the rag over the cut on her cheek.

"It was a dirty move, Kid," Brody said. "He could've taken us both out. You know we're not supposed to be doing that crap in practice." Brody acted as if he needed to explain Cass' actions.

Justin nodded, concentrating on holding the towel to her cheek.

Cass reached over and tightened her hand on Justin's arm. Brody was the only person they didn't need to hide their relationship from.

"He said something about wanting to meet your woman. What was he talking about?"

Startled, Justin eyes searched hers and the hand holding her chin became more of a caress than a hold. He sighed. Letting her hold the towel, he leaned against the car, folding his arms in front of him in a defensive gesture.

Cass pinned Brody with her stare. He shrugged and gave her an *I'm not talking* look.

Justin's mouth was tense. "Beau McCalister, now named 'The Terminator', is the man who caused my accident. He plagued me my entire Winston career. I don't know why, jealousy maybe, who knows—he made it a point to come after me any chance he got. Until finally..." His mouth turned hard and his nostrils flared. "I thought they banned him from racing, but I can see he's back. Like a sore you can't get rid of. He probably paid his way back, no doubt. Now it looks like he's playing the same game with you, Cass, and Brody." He pushed away from the car. "Time for you guys to get back out there and prove to him he's not going to scare you. Brody, let Cass draft, then come in. We're going to practice pitting."

Brody saluted and left to climb into his car.

Cass approached Justin, taking his bruised and bleeding hand. Her head down, she took the towel from her cheek and wrapped it around his hand. Her fingers lingered over his. "Your poor hand," she murmured. Then, feeling as if the words were torn out of her throat, she said, "This guy scares me."

Justin twisted her around so she was against the car, his back blocking any view of them. He sandwiched her between his arms.

"Good. Be scared. He's very dangerous. Don't take your eyes off of him. He came up so fast on you today I didn't even see him. Always know where he is. He will side-swipe you at any chance he gets, don't ever doubt that. And don't let him pull you into fighting with him like he did today. He knows it'll look bad for your sponsors and…" he moved closer, his body almost touching hers, "my hand is fine. It was worth every scratch to watch him go down."

She smiled and lowered her eyes to their linked hands. Running her thumb over his knuckle, she felt him shudder.

"God," he said, his voice husky, "do you know how bad I want to kiss that fear from your face right now? Do you?"

Her eyes met his. The desire she saw set to rest her fears that he didn't still want her. With a twist of his hand, he entwined all five fingers with hers. She cleared her throat rather than moan when his traced her wrist, then rested his fingers on her rapid pulse. His eyes closed. Out of the corner of her eye, she caught a movement as Lee approached them. She quickly disengaged her hand and started to get into the car.

"Are you hurt?" Lee asked.

"No, I think Justin took the brunt of the punishment this time."

Justin raised his towel-bandaged hand to Lee. Cass lifted herself up and slid into the car. Buckling herself in, she watched Lee and Justin.

"I got a call from Mrs. K. Apparently, this little episode is already on the news and she wasn't too happy."

Cass grimaced and leaned her head against the back head support.

"Great, I think Beau just won and I fell right into his trap." She hit her hand against the steering wheel, swearing.

"That's okay, just don't let it happen again. I think Justin saved us with his speech. Anyway, she wants to see us all Thursday morning at her hotel."

Cass lifted her head and rolled her eyes.

Justin shrugged. "Don't worry about it, Cass. Do what you do best, and I'll deal with the rest." He leaned in the window and checked her harness, smiling at her exasperated expression.

She reluctantly smiled back, unable to resist him—even when he used her own words against her. She slid on her helmet and hooked up her gear. Justin stepped away from the car when she flipped the ignition switch. Giving them both a thumbs up, she swept onto the raceway.

A few minutes later she heard Justin's voice in her ear. "Keep an eye out for Beau. He's on the third turn. Keep it below 180 mph on turn two, it banks at eighteen degrees, and maintain your line. Brody is coming out of turn two."

Yes. We're back in business.

~

And so they continued for the next three days, Justin watching Cass' back, Cass watching her front. Cass passed NASCAR's scrutiny and approval to become an official NASCAR Cup driver. She was now official.

~

Thursday morning, Cass met Justin, Lee and Brody in the lobby of Mrs. Kingsdale's hotel. She had dressed carefully in a stylish business suit, smart yet sexy, trying to appear the professional that Mrs. K expected. This would be her first meeting with her mysterious sponsor.

"Wow!" Justin whistled as he took her arm to escort her to the elevator. "You look fantastic."

Lee piped up his two cents. "Ditto."

She smiled at both of them and clung to Justin's arm, hugging it to her side. He patted her arm with his hand, and reached up to touch the bruise on her cheek.

His expression turned fierce. "Does it hurt?" he asked, stroking the skin around the cut.

"No." She nodded at his bruised hand. "Does yours?"

He grinned. "Um, a little."

She released his hand and bobbed up and down of the balls of her toes, attempting to dispel her nervousness. Lee punched in the floor number and the metal doors slid closed.

"Relax," Justin said stroking her arm.

"I know, let you do your job and all of that." She sighed and sucked in a deep breath. "I know."

Lee put an arm around her shoulders and squeezed. "Don't worry, we won't let the big bad executive eat you."

She laughed. "I know, you guys. I hate this kind of thing."

The elevator opened to the penthouse. All three stepped into the foyer, then across to a door that led into the main suite.

Justin knocked on the door. Cass felt like she was asking for entrance into the White House.

A man about ten years older than Justin opened the door. He was slender and looked as if he could be on the cover of *Yachting Magazine*. "I'm glad to meet you all. I'm Albert Kingsdale, Margaret's son." He nodded at Lee, shaking his hand. "Mr. Gray, I'm impressed with the team you have assembled." He quickly turned to Cassandra, taking her hand, and covering it with his other hand. "And Ms. Jamison, it is indeed a pleasure to meet you. Your dossier impressed me. After reading Lee's reports on your progress, I'm even more impressed."

"Thank you." He cradled her hand longer than she thought necessary. It gave her a little bit of the creeps.

Justin slipped forward, forcing Kingsdale to break his grip. Kingsdale frowned at Justin, and moved to Brody. "And Mr. Carmichael, your driving also needs noting. I'm also impressed with your record. The team is in good hands if you have to drive."

Brody shook his hand. "Appreciate your confidence, sir."

Kingsdale shifted to Justin. "And last but certainly not least, our legendary Mr. Steed." He shook Justin's hand. "I followed your career and was sorry to see you drop out of NASCAR. I am ecstatic that we were able to pull you back in, even if it is to coach our little lady here to victory."

Justin shrugged, as if the compliment slid off his back. "I appreciate the opportunity."

"Now, let's go in and meet my mother."

Albert led them to an office toward the back of the suite. Behind an oak desk sat the renowned Margaret Kingsdale, a small, gray-haired woman, immaculately groomed and dressed, looking much younger than her sixty-five years. She rose when they approached, gesturing queen-like to indicate they should sit. Cass shuddered, feeling Mrs. Kingsdale's power. This woman was a legend. She sat.

Mrs. K eased back in her chair. "So pleased you could all make it." Her gaze locked on Cass. "Yes, you're as beautiful in person as your picture."

Cass blushed at the compliment.

Mrs. K laughed. "Splendid. She even blushes."

Cass felt herself blushing more furiously. She guessed her face looked like a cherry mess.

"The primary reason for this meeting," Mrs. K continued, "is to inform you of your sponsorship schedule." She nodded at Albert.

He jumped to pick up small binders with the fuchsia Lovely logo on the front. Like a schoolboy passing out papers for the teacher, he handed one to everyone.

"Lee and Mr. Carmichael, you remain on the sidelines as Mr. Steed and Cassandra complete the publicity events." Mrs. K opened her binder, and so did the others.

Reading the schedule, Cass sucked in her breath. Television interviews, talk shows, mall appearances, commercial shootings, and corporate dinners ... the list was endless. It took twenty minutes alone for Mrs. K to review the ruthless nine-month publicity schedule. Then she moved on to their script and sound bites. The sponsor's name was to be used discreetly, but Lovely Cosmetics should be mentioned each time a team member opened his or her mouth. After an hour of instructions on what to say, what to wear, and where to be, Cass' mind spun.

"Now, I'll ask Mr. Gray, Mr. Carmichael and Albert to leave. I have some information to discuss with Mr. Steed and Cassandra only."

Lee, Brody and Albert jumped up at her command and departed. Mrs. K turned her attention to Cass and Justin, both sitting on a very uncomfortable, professional office couch with stiff cushions.

"Justin, if I may call you that." She paused while Justin nodded. "And Cassandra, I'd like you to watch something with me." She pressed a button and a TV screen lit up on the wall. She pressed another button, producing the sounds and visual of NASCAR *Today*, the show that covered current race happenings. The announcers were discussing Cass and Justin.

"This was the scene today at the Daytona Super Speedway pre-race practice," a smooth male voice said. The screen expanded to a visual of the raceway and The Terminator coming up fast on Cass' car.

"Beau 'The Terminator' McCalister pulled a bump and run on Cassandra Jamison, causing her to lose control of her car, spinning into the apron and landing in the end field. The strange thing is pre-race practices are not usually the place for bumps and scrapes. It's clear The Terminator was gunning for the young Ms. Jamison." The scene played out when Cass chased down Beau for the confrontation, then moved through Cass' fight with Beau, and Justin landing the ending punch. It shifted to Justin wiping Cass' face and standing very close to her. Justin's back blocked the camera from filming her holding his hand, Cass noted with relief.

The announcer's voice came back on. "There's more to this story than meets the eye, folks. Let's take you through the history here. That's right, the man you see attending young Jamison is none other than the NASCAR Kid." A picture of a handsome, young Justin appeared on the screen. He was sitting on top of his car in the middle of a celebration.

"Justin Steed, nicknamed the NASCAR Kid, was an incredible success on the NASCAR Winston circuit." There were flashes of Justin driving on various tracks, bumping, grinding, and spinning with hits taken from the #45 car. Cass' hand joined with Justin's. He squeezed, acknowledging her support.

"Justin was haunted by Beau McCalister during his six-year career. This didn't stop the NASCAR Kid, who went on to win five championships. Steed was well known and admired, not only for his exceptional driving abilities but also for his Kids Against Drugs campaign. It's one of the few programs successful in keeping many of America's children off the streets and away from drugs." A picture showed of Justin with his arms around several kids in front of the building of a rehab center.

"Unfortunately, NASCAR's most grievous loss happened November 11th, the last race of Steed's sixth season at the Atlanta Speedway." The screen flashed to the race they discussed and Justin's hand tightened painfully on Cass'. The race played out with Beau crashing into Justin's bumper, causing it to fly off the car. Justin started swerving on the backstretch, trying to get control of the car, when Beau moved up onto his left side and forcefully pushed him into the wall on the turn. Both Justin's tires blew and a chain reaction started. His car skid and flipped violently over and over at a devastating speed. The car scraped down the front stretch, the gas tank catching on fire and flames bursting around the car.

Justin stared at the screen, taking in deep breaths, gripping Cass' hand so hard her fingertips started to numb. Ignoring her squished fingers, she brought up her other hand to cover his. Mrs. K was watching the screen.

Finally, the scene ended with people tearing a bleeding, broken Justin from the car. Justin's hand reached over and he clutched his arm, as if he could still feel the break.

"Yes, folks, it's painful to watch. The accident ended the career of a great driver and man, a devastating loss to our sport. Beau McCalister was suspended for three years after the incident and is back this year, it seems with a vendetta. Justin Steed hasn't been heard from in three years, but it seems beautiful Cassandra has lured him back into action." The scene flipped to Justin wiping Cass' cheek. Watching, she could see his lips moving, as if he was trying to calm her.

"Now it seems that Beau has his sights set on Justin's protégé, Cassandra Jamison. Although not one of first females to make it into the circuit, she's certainly the most promising." A clip was shown of Cass practicing at Daytona.

"Cassandra Jamison, a Montana stock car racer and more than just a pretty face, has been training with Steed for the past six months at his home base in Tucson. It's obvious by her driving style that her skills are equal if not better than the Kid's. Her backup driver, Brody Carmichael, is also a well-respected driver. Their team manager is Lee Gray and their chief mechanic is Darrin Jacks. Folks, this makes for a dangerously competitive team for any other NASCAR competitors. Understandably, McCalister feels threatened, but his methods leave much to be desired and I'm sure NASCAR officials will be watching him closely. Jamison's sponsor, Lovely Cosmetics, should be proud of the team they have assembled. We commend them for backing a woman in the male-dominated world of NASCAR. We'll be following this team closely to see where they end up next. Tomorrow is qualifying for the Lovely Cosmetics team. Let's see how well Cass' time matches those of The Terminator as the countdown to the first event continues. And to the Kid—welcome back. Stay tuned."

Mrs. K pulled a cigarette from her gold case and lit it. Taking a long drag, she turned her chair and faced them. Cass released Justin's hand.

"So it begins."

Justin stood and began pacing. "So it seems."

"The chemistry between you two is undeniable. I expect you to exploit that as much as you can. You will attend all events together. However, you will not enter into any type of public affair. Others might be stupid as to what's happening between the two of you, but I am not."

Justin stopped pacing and faced the wall, his back to Mrs. K and Cass.

Mrs. K continued, "Your perceived availability to the other sex is essential. People must be able to think that they have a chance at catching both of you. That's part of the advertising—and part of their fantasy. The more they think of you, the more they will buy. Do you both understand?"

Justin remained silent.

Cass jumped up. "We understand. We both appreciate the opportunity you've given us." She stuck out her hand, hoping the interview was concluded. Any minute she expected Justin to tell Mrs. K what to do with her instructions.

Mrs. K shook Cass' hand, smiling at her. "I hope you do, Cassandra." She waved at her with a dismissing motion.

Cass grabbed Justin's arm, tugging him out of the office.

"Justin!" Mrs. K's imperious voice interrupted their departure. "Have I made myself clear?"

Justin nodded. "Crystal."

Cass dragged him out the door. Entering the elevator she punched a floor, hoping she could find an empty room. She could feel the tension running through Justin's body. He was breathing hard and his movements were stiff. The elevator door slid open. Peering from side to side, Cass tugged him along the hall, trying to find an empty room where he could let out his anger. The place seemed fairly deserted. There were several trashcans on rollers, as if the floor was getting a good cleaning. Seeing a supply room, Cass shoved him inside the small room and closed the door. Flipping on the light, she released him and crossed her arms in front of her.

Justin turned his back on her. He reached out his arms out and laid them on the shelves, gripping them. Dropping his head, he breathed deeply. Cass didn't know if his reaction was from watching the crash or Mrs. Kingsdale's orders, but he was having a hard time controlling his emotions. Walking up behind him, she slowly wrapped her arms around his middle. Sliding her body against his, she rested her cheek against his back. She stayed that way for a few minutes, trying to offer him the support he needed but wouldn't ask for. It was so good to be next to him again. She had wanted to touch him in the worst way, since that day at his house.

"Every time I see that crash, it takes a little more of my soul," he finally admitted. "What the hell am I doing here?"

Cass moved her hand along his back to his neck, trying to knead away the tension. "I know."

"Every day I feel the ridges of the scars from the accident, and sometimes I get so angry." He pounded his fist into the shelves to emphasize his point.

Cass didn't dispute his anger. She gave him comfort. She ran her hands over his back, caressing him, her fingers soothing his tight muscles. He began to relax, a slow loosening of the muscles. His head came up and he glanced over his shoulder. His tortured expression meshed with hers. He stared into her tear-filled eyes. Moaning her name, he turned to fold her into his arms. She couldn't resist his pull. Against her better judgment she leaned into him.

"God, Cass, I've missed holding you so much." His voice was rough but his lips softly caressed her neck. Pulling back, he stared into her face. His hands came up to frame her cheeks, wiping the lone tear away that had escaped.

"Don't," he whispered, running his fingertips under her eyes. "Don't cry for me, it's not worth it." His hands splayed and moved over her face. He shifted closer, his scent engulfing her, his mouth hovering close to hers.

"It *is* worth it, Justin. You are worth it," she said in a low voice, her eyes straying to his lips. He was worth it, in her mind. She had wanted to comfort him; however, his smell, the feel of him, the bunching of those muscles under her fingers were her undoing.

"Cass, I've tried to stay away from you, to give you space, I wasn't sure how you felt … about that night." His hands strayed from her face into her hair, massaging her scalp. It was the first time he had talked about that night and she was stunned that he doubted her feelings about what had happened.

"I won't let that woman," his head jerked toward Mrs. K's office, "tell me that I can't have a relationship with you. I can't stay away from you. Please tell me it's not just me—because I can't wait any longer to be with you." His lips hovered over hers as he waited for her response.

Not just him, what the hell is he talking about?

"Justin, you fool." She smiled when his lips tightened. She ran her hands through his hair, locking onto the back of his head. "How could you doubt my feelings about that night or about you?" She slowly raised her starving lips to meet his in a gentle kiss. His hands tightened in her hair. "That night was the most incredible night of my life. Better than any race I've ever won, more wonderful than I could ever imagine." She drew forward again and kissed him.

His lips moved against hers. "God, Cass," he breathed, hugging her to him. She could feel his erection against her stomach. He ran kisses along her jaw and then whispered seductively in her ear. "At night, when I close my eyes, I see you. I see your naked body against mine, I feel the touch of your hot skin against mine, I feel the taste of your lips against my lips, and I remember, Cass."

He kissed her again, his words inducing a seductive trance in Cass that went beyond the physical. She shut down her doubts. Who cared about their professional relationship? She wanted him inside her in the worst way, an elemental urge beyond reason—the emotions pushed her forward. "I remember what it felt like to be buried inside you, remember the feel of your silky legs wrapped around me, of my cock touching your womb." He shifted her against the back wall of the room, and he lifted her legs around him, pressing his penis against her.

Cass moaned in response to his words. She was thoroughly aroused, hot and dripping; she creamed in response to his touch. Justin slid his hands up her skirt. Placing them inside her pantyhose, he cupped her ass. "I remember our movements together." He rotated his hips, circling into her. He kissed her, not a gentle kiss this time, but a hot, possessive one. His tongue invaded her mouth, pulsing in and out to match the rotation of his hips. The touch of his tongue against her sent her over the edge.

"Then I wake up, trembling all over with desire, and realize you're not there. And I don't like it." He pulled one hand back and worked on his pants. Cass dropped her legs, her shoes thumping to the carpeted floor, so she could help him. Seconds later, his dick fell hard and aroused into her hands. He groaned when she cupped him, her hand caressing his balls. He pulled back to help her remove her nylons, then had her legs up and around him.

"I have a proposal for you," he said as he slowly entered her. He quieted her cry with his mouth as he continued to rotate against her, sending her head arching back. He kissed the pulse at her neck. Cass tried to register what he was saying but the feel of his huge dick buried inside her made it difficult for her to process anything, beyond his cock. His voice lowered to a whisper. "I propose that outside the track, in private, we are together in every way. That you sleep with me, that you shower with me, that you eat with me, that we spend every spare minute with each other. What do you say?" He paused to allow her to respond.

She ran her hands over his shoulders, shifting in his arms, plunging him deeper into her. It had been six months since she had seated him in her body, six long months without his hard dick, six lonely months. She had almost forgotten how amazing, how big and hard he felt, sliding into her. She tightened the walls of her vagina. He closed his eyes in response and his body began to move.

"Yes," she cried out as he set a rhythm that sent her over the edge of sanity. Her orgasm came fast and strong. He silenced her cries again with his mouth as he moved frantically against her, following her, spilling into her. His cry matched hers. He made one final push, his breathing heavy. Their immediate desire sated, he leaned his forehead against hers, holding her as if he never wanted to let her go. If she could keep him between her legs forever, it wouldn't be long enough.

"Yes, what?" he said between pants.

"Yes, we'll spend as much time as we can together." She felt his smile. He allowed her legs to slide to the floor.

"I'm sorry, Cass, I didn't mean to do this ... like this. I wanted you for so long, so much, I guess..." He shrugged his shoulders. "I lost control."

She smiled, and laughed at his little boy expression, a combination of guilt, sheepishness and pure male satisfaction. She helped him put himself together. When they finished, Justin drew her into his arms, gently kissing her lips. She ran her hands over his face. She wanted to eat him alive.

"I think we both lost control." She laughed at the fact that they were in a supply cabinet, two floors down from Mrs. K's office, making love like a couple of love-struck teenagers.

"Do you realize how badly we defied Mrs. K's order? I feel like a kid who's been out past her curfew."

He laughed with her, pulling back so he could look into her eyes. His laugh stopped, a muscle in his cheek twitching. "Screw Mrs. Kingsdale, no one will ever keep me from what's mine."

"So, I'm yours again, huh?" She ran a finger down his chest and she smiled at his possessiveness. She'd always been independent, but now she actually enjoyed being claimed by Justin Steed. It gave her a certain feminine satisfaction to know she could reduce a man of Justin's stature to a primitive level.

His lips took hers in a possessive kiss. "Do you doubt it?" he asked, his lips suspended over hers.

"Not one bit," she said with confidence, tasting those sensual lips.

He smiled, his hands running down her back to cup her rear. She could feel her heart speeding up and her arousal returning. The doorknob rattling cooled her. Justin swung his eyes to the locked door. He turned back to her and gave her a quick kiss.

"Let's move this to another location."

"Justin, what about practice today?"

"Practice is cancelled today in light of the fact you have to qualify tomorrow." He unlocked the door.

"Uh huh, I suspect some selfish motives here," Cass said, laughing as Justin opened the door and zoomed past the surprised janitor, Cass in tow.

"Sorry, got lost."

When they entered the empty elevator Justin had that predatory look again, his eyes smoldering. "Suspect all you want, practice is cancelled." He joined their hands and stepped in closer. "I have another ride in mind for you."

Cass chuckled all the way back to the hotel.

Chapter Nine

Daytona International Speedway, Dayton, Florida
Race 3, Daytona 500

"Keep it tight, Beau is right next to you, second pole. Watch him." Justin adjusted his headset while he sat up high in the Crew Chief position above the pits.

"Okay, got it." The tightness of her voice made him wince. *Oh man, she is tense.*

"Okay, Cass, sit back and enjoy the ride. There are two hundred laps in this race; we have a long, tough day ahead of us."

"Easy for you to say. You're lounging in the pits. Come out here and join the fun and see if you can sit back and take it easy." She sounded more relaxed, with an almost-smile in her voice as she teased him.

"You know I would if I could, babe."

"I know, Kid."

"You're in a great position. If you can stay there you've got it made. Have I told you, you did an incredible job in qualifying?" He knew they had one lap to go before start and this type of banter helped her relax before the race started.

"No, but thanks. I'm not the only one on this team, babe." She answered with laughter in her voice.

"Whoops, sorry," he accepted her warning for the pet name. "Okay, get set. Lee, I want your eyes on Beau. Keep it tight, Cass, and do your thing."

Simultaneous voices ricocheted in his ear as the green flag flew. The volume at the raceway accelerated beyond normal levels of hearing. He didn't have time to worry.

~

"He's coming up on your right." Cass heard Lee's voice in her ear. Lap 180. They had finished a tire change after a yellow caution flag and had been given the green flag to re-start the race. She'd managed to maintain third place throughout the race.

Cass was hot, tired, her car was battered and she was definitely losing tolerance for Beau's constant bumping and scraping.

"You've got to protect your right side," Justin warned in her ear. "If he hits that front tire again, you could lose it and we'll be out." His voice grew harsh. "Moving up—directly off your right rear."

Her hands jerked on the wheel when Beau jammed into her rear. She felt her front left tire break loose from the track as she skidded. She jerked toward the apron, working hard to gain control.

"God damn it!" she said. "I'm moving high on the next turn to pass number two. Lee, I'm going to try and put some room between me and this joker. If I let him get any closer he's going to kill me. How am I looking?"

"You're good, keep it clean, and be careful."

That was all the information she needed. Coming up on the tri-oval turn, she flawlessly and quickly moved out from behind the number two car. Hitting the accelerator, she fought the g-forces pulling her toward the wall. Her hands straining, she maintained her position on the turn, passing the second position car and dropping down in front of him on the stretch.

"Lee, where is he?" Cass glanced quickly in her mirror, seeing a blur of cars close behind her.

"He's blocked, bumped back to fourth position, five seconds behind."

"You're good," Justin said. "Stay where you are. You've got nineteen to go, your gas is good and you have two new tires. You're set."

Justin's reassurance calmed her racing heart. She had been dodging Beau for two hours. Her concentration and patience were both waning. She had far exceeded her stress level fifty laps prior. Tears streamed down her face as she concentrated on holding her position. Her nose was running and her throat was dry. She sniffed, hoping her condition wasn't coming over the microphone. There was so much tension centered on this race, she needed to release it somehow. She knew the public couldn't see her tears. With her full-face helmet and dark visor, all the in-car camera could see was her helmeted visage jerking with the car.

"How you doing? Eighteen to go." Justin's low calming voice broke into her agony and self-pity.

"A little stressed out right now. Where's Beau?" Her voice cracked with rawness and fatigue.

"He's blocked, you're fine. Maintain. You don't have to win. You're fine where you are. We're watching Beau like a hawk. We'll tell you if he makes a move."

Feeling less likely to fall apart before the end of the race, Cass kept her sights on the car in front of her and, as much as she could, beside her. At this stage, other desperate drivers got brash and this was the most dangerous part. Most of the cautions and wrecks happened when it came down to the line as reckless drivers tried to change positions, especially this race, the Superbowl of the NASCAR races.

Lee's voice boomed over her headset. "There's a caution behind you, three seconds back, yellow flag, debris on the roadway, keep clear."

"Come in," Justin said. "We'll adjust that right front tire. Your position is secure."

"Justin."

"Yup."

"I need some Kleenex or something, all right?" Cass was embarrassed to ask, but her nose was running so bad it was starting to distract her.

"Okay." His businesslike answer had her sighing in relief.

"Lee, am I clear for the pits?"

"Watch to your left ... there, okay, you're clear."

She pulled to her L position. Several crew members ran out to check her tire. Justin appeared at her window, offering her a tissue. She shoved it into the opening of her helmet and wiped as much of the tears and her nose as she could. He watched her with that *are you okay* expression. She shoved the Kleenex back at him, not something she'd usually do, but she normally wasn't driving a loaded car in one of the most important races of the season.

"I'm okay." She gave him the thumbs up.

"Go, go, go!" he yelled.

She whipped out back onto the track. "Where am I, Lee?"

"The debris is clear, you're back into position. Beau's in fourth position now, he'll be closer."

Justin's voice came on. "Your right side is a little more secure. Still protect it. The hit you took at lap fifty-seven left it vulnerable. You have eighteen laps to go. Beau will try to force a conflict now that he's closer. Watch him."

She swore into the microphone, her patience snapping like a rubber band stretched too far. "I'm not paid to watch him, God damn it, that's what you guys are for. I'm trying to drive here."

There was silence. She sighed at her outburst. She was losing control. "Sorry," she apologized. That was all she could think to say as she concentrated on lining up.

"We'll watch him," Justin said.

~

Twenty minutes, six cautions and four hits later from Beau had Cass ready to scream and drive off the track.

"Justin, if he hits me one more time, I swear I'll flip this car myself and put myself out of my misery."

"Cass, three to go. You have got to maintain your control." His stern voice calmed her agitation. "You're in third position, the field is clear. Beau is in front of you, babe. You're set, maintain your position. Just maintain. Okay?"

"Got it."

Cass concentrated on the two drivers in front of her, one being Beau. She maintained her position for the remaining two laps and, amazingly enough, no further cautions impeded them.

As they rounded the last lap, Cass drove up behind Beau's car. Coming out of the turn, she eased up beside him, pushing him high toward the wall.

"Cass, for God's sake, what the hell are you doing?" Justin yelled. "Get away from him. Back off."

Cass ignored him as Beau jammed back onto her right side. Her hands jerked as she tried to jam him back. Around the last curve, she felt her right side shaking and she changed tactics, whipping around the back of Beau's car. The instant Beau moved inward to gain more speed, Cass banked around the left, jammed him with her left side and passed him. They took the checkered flag, her car in second position and Beau's third.

Did I just take second place in the Daytona 500?

She pulled into the pits. Stopping, she tugged off her helmet and grabbed her fuchsia Lovely Cosmetics hat. She unhooked her seatbelts, and the crew was pulling her out of the car, hugging her. Second place didn't get quite the press of the winner, but it felt great. The burliest crew members spun her around and deposited her on top of the hood of the car. As her eyes searched for Justin, a microphone was shoved in her face.

"Ms. Jamison, how does it feel to be the first woman to take second place in the Daytona 500?" the reporter asked.

"I imagine the same way it feels to a man." She smiled at the camera and the reporter. He smiled back and laughed.

Cass raised her hands, gesturing to the crew around her. "The real thank you goes to Lovely Cosmetics and this group, Justin Steed, Lee Gray, Brody Carmichael, Darrin Jacks, and the rest of the Lovely Cosmetics team that made this happen. I'm only the driver." She smiled, finally spying Justin resting against the pit wall, his arms crossed. His expression looked grave instead of happy, as if he were one black flower in a field of sunny yellows.

She beamed at him. She wasn't going to let him spoil the moment. Pointing at him, she looked at the cameras.

"Of course, a special thanks to my wonderful crew chief, Justin Steed." All cameras and eyes turned toward him. She crooked her finger, motioning for him to come over. His surprised expression swung to the cameras. He pushed away from the wall and stalked through the crowd toward her like an angry lion moving up on his prey. When he reached the car, she placed her arm around him, hugging him closer.

"He deserves a gold medal for putting up with an ornery driver like me." She smiled at the camera, then at Justin.

As if he saw the apology in her eyes, she felt the tension ease from his bunched muscles. He grinned at the camera, and her wonderful day became more wonderful.

He has a killer smile.

"We're happy that we had a safe, successful race," Justin said. "I want to thank the team and Lovely Cosmetics for their support. Cass is modest. We all know what a vital role she played in today's important race."

More questions where thrown their way. Justin answered each one patiently. He handled the press as smoothly as a newly waxed car. Looking at his sensuous face as he talked, she sometimes forgot to breathe.

"What's the goal of this team?" a reported asked.

Cass took the question. "The goal, gentlemen and ladies," she jumped off the car and, arm in arm, began to walk away with Justin, then turned and absently finished her answer, "is to win."

She smiled and flipped her hair. Laughing, she continued to walk, her arm anchored through Justin's. The crew was beginning the clean up before starting on the long celebration of their almost victory.

Justin laughed. "You're a natural actress."

She shrugged her shoulders. "Among other things."

Cass stopped when they reached the rented car. "Sorry I got grumpy, in the car. What can I say, the job's hell." Her gaze dropped. She told herself it wasn't that she was too embarrassed to face him. She was suddenly really interested in her shoes.

He opened the door for her and quickly followed her in. He drew her hand to his mouth for a slow kiss to her palm, and her heart accelerated. "You'll be the death of me someday," he said. "When you get reckless and angry like you did at the end of the race, my heart stopped beating. You've got to keep calm in that car. It's not like you're driving to Wal-Mart." His sad expression met her eyes over their intertwined hands.

She nodded. "I'll try. It's how I am."

He sighed, releasing her hand. "I know. Get back to the hotel and get some rest. Tonight we have a corporate dinner. I'll pick you up at eight. I've got to stay and help the crew."

She closed her eyes and rested her head on the back of the seat. She felt his hand run down her face, and he told the driver where to take her.

~

Slow, sensual, drugging kisses running along Cass' neck woke her. She was sprawled flat in the bed, still wearing her fuchsia racing uniform. She smiled when she smelled his masculine scent. Only one man could stir her into this level of creamy arousal.

"Justin," she said, her voice thick with sleep. As she started to reach for him, she realized why he'd woken her. She groaned. "Is it time?"

The warm mouth withdrew from her neck and she felt the bed next to her lean in as he sat down. His hand gently stroked her hair. Cass sighed in pleasure.

"Yes, you need to get ready. Mrs. Kingsdale sent over a dress. It's hanging in the closet."

She rolled over, looking at him, her heart momentarily stalled. "Justin," she breathed, her gaze trailing hungrily over him. He wore a black tux, his white tux shirt unbuttoned and gaping open, giving her a glimpse of his beautiful, muscular chest. He was cleanly shaven, his hair tamed enough to look so sexy she wanted to mess it up. His bedroom brown eyes were smiling at her reaction.

"Will I pass?" he asked, drawing her forward for a quick kiss.

"Pass? I'd say you're at the top of the class. You look fantastic." She reached forward to brush a piece of fuzz off his shoulder, then groaned and hauled herself from the bed. She swayed with fatigue.

Justin was up, instantly cradling her in her arms.

"Hey there, babe, are you okay?" he asked, concern written on his face.

She moved forward into his embrace and, for a moment, she placed her head against his heart and closed her eyes. His hand stroked her hair, and she paced her breathing with his steady heartbeat. A beautiful, slow, burning desire began to penetrate her thoughts. She held on, never wanting to release him.

"I'm fine, a little sleepy. Please push me toward the shower."

He laughed, and helped her undress. Although he behaved himself, his hands lingered on her naked flesh. She recognized the hungry look on his face. They hadn't made love since the day they met Mrs. Kingsdale. They'd been so busy, Cass fell into bed every night in pure exhaustion.

"Justin, I recognize that look, and if we didn't have to be somewhere…"

He groaned and stepped back, raising his hands. "I know, but God, Cass." He shook his head. "Okay, I'll check on Lee and Brody and leave you to…" He stopped mid-sentence when she moved into the bathroom and leaned over to start the shower. She glanced over and saw his eyes following her every move.

"Cass," he pleaded. He stepped behind her and ran his hand down her naked back, then pressed against her.

She felt an answering thrill but waved her hand at his agonized expression. Now it was her turn to be strong. "Go, Justin, or we won't go anywhere tonight."

He nodded and backed out of the bathroom. "Right, okay, I'm going." He stumbled over his feet, and she laughed.

"Go." Pointing to the exit, she stepped over to shut the bathroom door. As she reached up to put her hand against the door, he swept her into his arms.

Her heart slammed in her chest. His lips came down on hers, and he was devouring her, his mouth on hers, his hands running the length of her body.

"I need to love you," he murmured, his mouth leaving hers to run a damp, warm trail down the sensitive length of her neck, then downward yet. Closing in on her nipples, he licked and nipped.

Cass melted, then surrendered. "Yes," she whispered. "Yes." She couldn't deny him.

She ripped his unbuttoned shirt off him, tossing it to the floor. She couldn't think, only feel.

He attacked her with his gentle kisses, licking and bathing her skin, her nipples. Then his mouth traveled lower down her body. He dropped to his knees before her and anchored his mouth on her vagina.

Cass arched in pleasure. She was on fire, her body tingling with sensation from her toes to the top of her head. He grabbed her ass, tilted her hips and feasted.

God, was anything better than this man's mouth on her?

Her knees shook, her breath hitched, her body a slave to his mouth. She cried out when her orgasm hit her. Moaning, she grabbed his hair, her hand tunneling through the silken darkness. She pressed his face against her as he licked her like a Popsicle, sucking up every last bit of her wetness.

Tugging on his upper arms, Cass guided him up. She burned with a need to return the pleasure he'd given her. He kissed her neck, her jaw. The scent of her cum tweaked her senses as he licked the corner of her mouth, sharing the wetness.

"Taste me," he said. "Taste us."

Cass accepted his tongue in her mouth and took him in. Reaching down, she opened his pants and ran her fingers along the top of his briefs. She needed to touch him. She craved him.

Pulling away, she ordered, "Drop them."

He chuckled and helped her take off his pants. All that was on her mind was taking his huge cock into her mouth and pleasing him the way he had her. She ran her hands down his back, over his hips. He had the most beautiful body, his skin soft yet rough, sprinkled with hair, his muscles defined and hard. His body was so different from her own. Running her hands over his tight ass, she reveled in the sensations, the ability to touch him at will, the fact that he was hers. Just stroking his body made her hot.

Guiding his hands, she anchored them to the vanity.

"Stay."

He looked like a happy bear that had just eaten the entire jar of honey.

"Gladly."

His smile turned into a groan when she dropped to her knees and began to suck his cock with a vengeance. She cupped his balls while guiding him into her mouth. Sucking, licking, nipping lightly, she worked on bringing him to orgasm. Pleasure, want, she needed him. The thrusting motion of his hips, his groaning and the clenching of his muscles egged her on. She applied herself to the task of loving his dick. She loved the taste and the feel of him.

His actions told her he was ready to burst. His hand fell from to vanity to the top of her head. Sweat glistened on his body. Cass took him deep into her mouth, her tongue swirling around his veined erection. He was beginning to pulse and thrust. His hand tightened on her hair, clenching to the point of pained pleasure.

"God, babe, I'm going to come."

Cass' enthusiasm grew. She was dripping wet with his excitement. She sucked him deep, in and out, her hand squeezing his balls. She wanted him to come for her and her only.

Suddenly he burst, spurting into her mouth. He yelled, his body bowed as he lunged forward. Cass took in his wetness. Licking, she cleaned and loved. He tugged her upward into his arms. Replacing his dick with his mouth, he kissed her as if he never wanted to stop. Cass wrapped her arms around his shoulders. Delving her hands into his hair, she kissed him back until he pulled away. After dropping a few more kisses on her jaw, he leaned back. Cass smiled at him. Now he looked like a very satisfied bear, one who didn't get just the jar of honey but the whole pot.

"It appears I managed to mess up your hair," she said.

He stroked her body with his rough, callused hands.

"That was my goal, you know."

Grabbing her ass, he yanked her against his body. "Was it?"

"Yes."

He turned them so they faced the mirror. Raising his eyebrows, he laughed. "You certainly did."

Cass ruffled his already messed hair. "Looks great."

"Ya think?" He released her and leaned over to start the shower. Cass' heart accelerated when his ass tightened. His

hard, sculptured ass was beautiful, a Michelangelo piece of work.
That ass will be the death of me.
"Come on, babe. I'll let you start from scratch."
Cass smiled when he hauled her into the shower.
Looks like we're going to be late.

~

Justin retrieved his tux jacket from his room, and strolled through the connecting door to Cass' room. The vision of loveliness in front of the mirror stopped him. He stood still, taking her in. Encased in a gold, curve-hugging dress, her blond mane pinned to the top of her head, was his girl. A girl despite the fact he had taken her multiple times. As he watched her, desire crashed through him and he wanted her again with a fierceness that was inhuman.
She is the sexiest woman. I could fuck her all night and not be satisfied.
Justin's heart began its familiar rapid pace since the day she rode into his life. He came up on her while she was applying what appeared to be a clear gloss on her lips. His arms came around her from behind, and she sucked in her breath, tensing in surprise. He bent his head, his lips caressing her long, sexy neck with feather light kisses. She relaxed and smiled at him over her shoulder.
Pulling her body against his, Justin's passion mounted. "You are the most beautiful woman I've ever met." He breathed against her neck, watching their wrapped forms in the mirror. He saw her eyelids lower, desire written on her face. He ran both of his hands down her hips, very slowly, and watched her eyes close as she leaned into him. Exhaling, she dropped her head against his chest. Her pleasure was his.

Looking at their images in the mirror, Justin saw her smile as he nibbled on her neck and ran kisses to her one bare shoulder. He slowly turned her around to face him, his lips moving to claim hers. Her arms twined around his neck.

The sound of the phone broke the spell. Justin reached for it and Cass' hand came out to stop his.

"This is my room, remember."

"Whoops, right." When he was this close to her, the only thing he thought about was loving her.

She released his hand and leaned over to grab the phone, his arm still around her. She brought the receiver to her ear.

"Hello." Her musical voice flowed over Justin, soothing his mind. "Jewel, how's my favorite baby sister?" There was a pause, and she laughed. "I know you're my only sister, but you're still my favorite."

Justin nuzzled her neck.

"Thank you. I'll tell you, it was not an easy task. I was bawling like a baby at one point."

Justin hugged her tighter.

"A star? I don't think so. A few minutes of national TV coverage does not make someone a star."

Justin caressed the smooth skin of her shoulder. She felt like warm silk.

"That gorgeous man was Justin, my crew chief." Her eyes strayed to his and he raised his eyebrows in question.

"Yes, he's taken," Cass said with a huge smile. "Yes, by me."

Justin smiled back.

"Jewel, I'm shocked that you would ask me a question like that."

Justin planted a sensual kiss on Cass' neck.

"Oh, yes." Cass breathed against the phone. "Yes, he's here, now."

Justin shifted to her other ear, gently blowing. She reached up and lightly slapped him. Smiling, he pulled back slightly, but didn't release her.

"Brody? Yes, that's his real name."

Justin stopped smiling and scowled.

"Yes, he's available."

He grinned and started to distract her again. He drew her hand to his chest, then ran it down until she cupped his arousal. His hard cock strained toward her palm, as if trying to escape his tux slacks.

She held the phone an inch away from her ear. Looking up at him, she asked, "Where will we be during spring break?"

Justin had to think about her question. Their schedule was so packed he needed to look at the appointment schedule to keep track.

"Virginia or Tennessee," he said as he rocked against her hard.

Her breath hitched, but she turned away, brining the phone back to her mouth. "I'll tell Lee that you'll be with us during spring break. He'll make all the arrangements, don't worry about anything."

Justin moved his hand around to her ass. He began massaging her.

That steady burn of desire was starting to consume him.

"I love you too, baby sister. See you soon." She dropped the phone.

Justin immediately claimed her lips. His tongue teasing hers, he sucked, licked, and settled in to take. If they never left the bedroom again, he would be immensely happy.

Jerking away from him, she scolded, "You're a menace, Justin Steed."

He laughed, then groaned at the knock on the door. "Yeah, but I'm your menace." He reluctantly released her. Crossing the room, he adjusted his pants to cover his erection before answering the door. Lee and Brody, dressed to the hilt, stood in the hall, their mouths tight with impatience.

"I thought we were leaving thirty minutes ago." Lee complained in the whining tone he used when he wanted to make a point.

Justin threw open the door, allowing them to enter. Brody and Lee saw Cass at the same instant. Both their bodies jerking forward, they bumped into each other. Brody stood straighter, and Lee gulped. "Oh, I see," Lee said.

Rolling his eyes at them, Justin picked up Cass' golden shawl and wrapped it around her shoulders. His hands lingered, caressing. He needed to touch her; it was a craving he couldn't deny. Realizing they needed to go, he grudgingly released Cass and stepped back.

Cass smiled at Lee and Brody's stunned faces, and Justin watched as she glided like a golden Macy's float toward the door. His eyes followed every sway of her luscious hips. Picking up a golden purse, she said, "Let's go, boys."

Brody and Lee stumbled after her like dogs in heat. Justin closed the hotel door, pocketed the key and leisurely came up from behind. Cass paused to let Lee and Brody pass, and wrapped her arm through his. He smiled. Out of this group of men, he was the luckiest one to have this woman attached to his arm.

On the way down the elevator, Cass asked Lee to arrange for her sister to join them during spring break. Lee nodded, although the way his eyes kept straying to Cass' cleavage when she leaned toward him, Justin wasn't sure he heard a word she said.

He growled. "Lee." Justin's sharp command brought Lee's eyes up to meet his. "Are you getting all of this?"

Stepping back, Lee nodded, his sheepish expression saying he got Justin's message that Cass was Justin's woman and Lee needed to pull up his eyes.

Cass continued to talk to him about Jewel's visit. When he looked at her again, his gaze remained above her neck.

Justin swung his gaze to Brody, who raised his hands in the universal sign of surrender, as if to tell him he already knew she was hands off. Justin nodded curtly.

His eyes wandered over Cass' slender hand clutching his arm. Without thought, in front of everyone, he laced his fingers into hers.

Still talking to Lee, she paused, and continued. Her fingers tightened on his. After their ride to the hotel they wouldn't get another chance to touch. Per Mrs. Kingsdale's instructions, they would have to maintain their distance yet still be together.

This shit is going to kill me.

A limo awaited them to take them to the Excelcius Hotel in the heart of the city. To show off the Lovely team, Mrs. Kingsdale had assembled an impressive roster of influential clients for an evening of dining and dancing. Justin locked hands with Cass, tucking her close to his side during the drive. He wasn't worried about what Lee and Brody thought. Both could be trusted and he guessed they had long ago figured out Justin and Cass were secretly together, in every way.

The ride was short and Lee and Brody launched out of the car upon arrival. Instead of sliding out to join them, Cass pulled Justin toward her.

"Justin."

"Yeah, babe?"

She ran her hand gently over his scarred face, her fingers delving into hair. His heart picked up a beat. She had this inane ability to make him rock hard at a moment's notice. All she needed to do was touch his face.

"Kiss me," she whispered as she slowly moved toward him.

"Gladly." He cupped his hand on her neck and drew her the additional three inches against his body. Staring into her eyes, he moved forward and consumed her lips, making them his. When the kiss ended, she was breathless. His thumb caressed her face, straying down to her lips. Outlining her mouth with his finger, he smoothed the spot where he had nipped. He leaned over and systematically licked that same spot, running his tongue around her lips.

He would never get enough of her. Even now he wanted to lick her from head to toe, then make slow, passionate love, all night long. A knock on the window made him turn his head. He glanced at Lee's fatherly expression.

She moaned and sighed. "Ah, damn. We have to go."

Reluctantly, he released her. "I know."

They both left the car to follow Brody and Lee. Cameras caught them immediately, blinding them, reporters everywhere. Justin reached back and guided Cass next to him.

"Mr. Steed, what do you have to say about the race today? What's your future strategy?"

"I'd say that our hope is to finish each race with a well running machine, a healthy driver, and few mistakes. That's how we hope to run this tour." Justin tightened his grip on Cass' arm, keeping her close.

"Ms. Jamison, how do you intend to deal with The Terminator and keep yourself from the same fate as the NASCAR kid?"

Cass' body language told Justin the question made her angry.

"I feel confident with my team and the support of our sponsor, Lovely Cosmetics," she said firmly. "I hope to have a clean season."

"Cass, Cass," other reporters yelled, trying to get her attention as Justin kept them moving along. "How do you respond to Beau McCalister's allegation that you're just a pretty face and won't last more than ten races?"

Justin scowled at the allegations. He was proud of Cass' answer.

"I'd say that I'm flattered that Mr. McCalister finds me attractive. However, as I said previously, I'm confident we will finish this season in a top position."

"Mr. Steed, there's been talk. Is there more than a crew chief, driver relationship between you and Ms. Jamison?"

Justin's jaw tightened and his gut clenched. "I'm not sure I need to respond to that."

"So you deny any other relationship with her?"

Justin began to answer when Cass cut in.

"Justin is a key member of my team and our relationship is as close as any driver and crew chief can be. Questions of any other type of relationship are degrading to both Justin and myself. I would appreciate it if you would refrain from reporting on issues that are not related to the race track." When Cass finished, several reporters' hands dropped, others murmured an apology, and one female reporter actually clapped.

Justin smiled. No one messes with my girl, he thought. As they walked toward the door, shouts of good luck came from the crowd.

He leaned over and whispered in Cass' ear, "Well done, babe, you put them in their place."

She smiled as they followed Lee and Brody into the dining room. When they entered, all eyes turned toward them and a quiet murmur wafted over the crowd, followed by a round of applause.

Satisfaction filled Justin. It was a golden moment for him, his girl, and his team. It couldn't get any better. He watched Mrs. Kingsdale approach, Albert trailing behind like a whipped puppy.

"Lee, Brody, Justin and Cass, I'm so glad you're here." Mrs. Kingsdale hooked her arm through Justin and Cass', sandwiching herself between them.

Justin snorted. He didn't recall the old biddy giving them a choice. In her usual queenly manner, she had commanded them to be there.

"I have some very important people I would like you to meet."

~

For the next two hours they circled the room, shaking hands and smiling so much that Cass thought her face was going to crack. They ate from the most unappealing buffet and finally, at the end of the long room, Mrs. K led them to a group of rough looking males. Cass recognized Beau McCalister at once.

"I took the liberty of inviting the top five drivers from the race to join us tonight, and they were kind enough to come."

Cass' eyes narrowed as she studied Beau. He lifted a half filled glass at her, his eyes glinting. Cass stood next to Justin, taking comfort from his nearness. She shook hands with the other drivers, whom she knew by name only. When it came to Beau, she pulled back her hand.

"Now, Cass, if I may call you that." Beau's slurring voice told her he was drunk, which could make the situation explosive.

Suddenly, Mrs. K took Justin's arm and steered him away from Cass, saying she had some people for him to meet. Justin looked over his shoulder, his stormy eyes meeting Cass'. She smiled to reassure him she'd be okay.

She turned back to the group. "Gentlemen, would you excuse us?" Cass' eyes locked on Beau's.

The other men moved away, obviously not wanting to be involved in their discussion. Cass grabbed Beau by the shoulder, then careened out of the dining room into a deserted catering hall, pulling him stumbling after her. In the hallway, she shoved him against the wall.

"No, you may not call me Cass. Matter of fact, I suggest you leave right now, and stay away from me." She was breathing hard, all of her anger centered on Beau.

"Now, Cass, that's not very ladylike," he slurred, juggling his glass. He swayed, trying to break her hold. She pushed him harder against the wall, freeing her rage.

I'd like to squash him like a bug.

"Listen, Beau, I don't know what your problem is, but you're not the only one who can start a vendetta. You either get off my ass or I will make your life miserable. I come from the raceways of Montana, and we take care of our own revenge. So don't think you scare me and don't think I won't bite back."

With a swish of her hand, she knocked the drink out of his grip. He watched the glass crash to the floor, glass shards flying. His mouth gaped open. Cass released his shoulder and brushed her hands together, as if she was brushing off dirt. "I think you've had enough to drink."

"Listen, you bitch…"

Cass cut him off, smashing her finger into his chest. "No, you listen, I've had enough of your bump and grind to last my whole career. I'm warning you, if you continue it's going to get ugly, because I'm not running anymore." She punctuated the remark with one more poke to his chest. "If it's war you want … I'm well armed and ready to rumble. So if you want your

NASCAR license suspended again, keep it up. I make a pretty convincing victim."

He stood perfectly still for a moment. She thought she glimpsed a seed of fear in his eyes, then it was quickly masked. He turned and strode back into the dining room mumbling, "Bitch." Cass followed and watched him leave the party.

She smiled. One accomplishment of the evening accounted for. Her searching gaze found Justin. He stood next to Mrs. K, his arms crossed, like a small child being scolded. He was clearly relieved when he spotted Cass, then Mrs. K took a death grip on his arm and whispered something to him. He nodded. She dropped his arm and left.

Justin approached Cass and swept her onto the dance floor. They stayed a respectful distance apart as he swayed her across the floor.

"What was she saying?"

He screwed up his face and, in a high falsetto voice, said, "Justin, you will not pursue them. That would appear the action of a jealous, overprotective lover, wouldn't it? I have already warned you about that, haven't I?"

Cass laughed at him, and sighed. "Justin, I hate this. I hate being in your arms but not..."

He tightened his hold slightly. "I know, babe, but tonight we are under the hawk eyes of Mrs. Kingsdale, who has already threatened me three times because I looked at you the wrong way."

"Oh, one of *those* looks. They are..." She paused, tilting her head, smiling, her voice taking on that honey sweet sexy quality she knew drove him crazy. "They are erotically sensual. Those looks make me think about another time and another place. Where we are alone, naked, and tasting each other, touching every inch we can. No wonder Mrs. K wants to outlaw your looks." Cass laughed when Justin stumbled, coughing to cover up his groan.

He released her. "Okay, that's it, I'm going to see how soon we can blow this joint."

Cass smiled and picked up on one of his words. "Blow, hmm." She placed a finger on her chin as if she were contemplating something. "Interesting choice of words, babe."

"You're killing me."

"I know, and you're doing the same to me by looking, so…"

"I'm going now." He nodded at her and quickly left.

~

Cass wandered, ending up at the drinking fountain. She smelled Justin's scent and felt his breath against her neck. "I think I found us a way out," he said.

She turned, smiling. "Lead the way."

He drew her hand into his large callused one and slowly tugged her toward the back of the room. Exiting into the same hall where she'd confronted Beau, he began pulling her down the hall. They popped out of a door leading to the lobby where Brody and Lee waited.

Cass felt ecstatic about leaving the party, as if she could cry with happiness. "I got her," Justin said, as if he had rescued a spy from the hands of the crooks. "Let's go."

Brody and Lee appeared to be relieved at leaving the party. The limo was waiting. They settled themselves on the wide seats.

"So, Cass, tell us," Lee said as the limo slid smoothly into traffic. "What did you say to scare Beau McCalister into running out of the party?"

"You noticed, huh?" She casually picked at her nails as if she didn't have a care in the world. She glanced sideways. Justin watched her, waiting for her answer.

"Well, I gave him a little old fashioned Montana warning," she said and finally looked up, smiling.

The whole car laughed. Justin hugged her closer.

"A Montana warning, huh," Lee repeated. "I don't even want to know what that is."

"Speaking of Montana ... Brody?"

Leaning back in his seat, Brody nodded. "Yes, ma'am?"

"When my sister's here for spring break, I was wondering if, while I'm practicing and such if ... well ... you could show her around."

Justin turned his head. Widening his eyes, he looked pointedly at her.

"You can count on me. If she's as beautiful as you are, I'm sure it won't be a burden." Brody rested his head back against the seat.

Cass recognized his exhaustion. She was experiencing the same feeling. They had been run ragged on the tour, one obligation after another, leaving them with a deep tiredness which never seemed to end.

"I'm sure you won't find her lacking in looks."

He grunted in response.

Cass hid her smile, feeling as if she'd set the wheels of love in motion. Jewel would be the perfect woman to tame the Texas charm of Brody.

Justin moved his mouth close to her ear. "I can't believe you."

She mouthed *what* and held up her hands. He wrapped his arm around her. Then he also laid his head back against the headrest. She looked at Lee who was shaking his head at her.

She mouthed *what* again. He smiled and hunkered down into his seat.

Cass leaned her head against Justin's shoulder; they took rest where they could get it these days.

Chapter Ten

April, Race 10
Martinsville Speedway, Martinsville, Virginia
Thursday, Practice Day

"Incredible." Brody's remark and his hand on Justin's arm stopped Justin from climbing into the Crew Chief's perch. He glanced at Brody's intent expression. Turning, Justin saw Lee walking down the pit area toward them. And strolling beside Lee was the second most beautiful woman Justin had ever seen. The woman resembled Cass in most ways but one. Instead of long, golden hair, the breeze blew back midnight black hair from her perfectly sculptured face.

As she approached, her head tilted to listen to Lee. Holding his arm, she smiled, an alluring smile, like Cass'. The closer she came the more beautiful they could see she was. Her classically shaped face was similar to Cass', but a little younger with her pert nose, her rose cheeks, and… Justin reined in his thoughts.

Jewel—for who else could she be but Cass' sister?—smiled at him and Brody. Justin looked over at Brody's mesmerized gaze staring into ice blue magnetic eyes, like Cass'. His hand over his mouth, Justin muffled a laugh at Brody's reaction.

Justin knew that sledgehammer in the heart moment, the same reaction he'd felt when he met Cass. Even though Justin admired Jewel's youthful beauty, his feelings for this woman were friendly, almost brotherly.

"Justin, Brody, meet Jewel Jamison, Cass' sister."

Justin shook Jewel's hand as Cass squawked in his ear. He put his hand up to the headset to indicate he was talking. Lee explained to Jewel that Justin was communicating directly with Cass.

"Justin, where're my track stats? I've asked four times. Are you sleeping over there?"

He smiled at Jewel, making a sign with his hand and pointing to the track where cars roared past each other, getting the feel of the curves and turns before tomorrow's race. Jewel smiled back and nodded.

"Cass, sorry, your sister just arrived. I got a little distracted."

"Ah, now I understand. Not too distracted, I hope."

He laughed. "No, babe, not too distracted."

"Is Brody dumbstruck?" Anticipation rang in her voice.

He glanced over at Brody who was holding Jewel's hand as if he never wanted to let go.

"I'd say that's an understatement."

She laughed. "Good, I'm coming in."

~

A few minutes later, Cass pulled into the pits. She slipped out of her gear, and jumped out of the car. Both women let out a scream and hugged each other in a bone-crushing embrace.

"Oh, baby sister, how I've missed you." Cass pulled away. "You haven't changed a bit, as beautiful as ever." She ran a hand down Jewel's hair.

Jewel laughed and hugged Cass again. "Neither have you, big sister."

Cass stepped back. "Have you met the crew?"

"Yes, Lee was kind enough to pick me up at the airport, and I've met Justin." She raised her eyebrows, wiggling them at her. "And Brody." She wiggled her eyebrows again, her face angled away from the men.

Cass put her arm around her waist and steered her toward Brody.

"I've got to finish up here. If you don't mind, Brody has already finished. I'll have him take you back to the hotel and then join you in say … two hours. You can unpack and get a little rest from the flight."

"That would be great!" Jewel said enthusiastically, and Cass suspected her sparkling eyes weren't at the prospect of a few hours' rest.

Cass turned to Brody. "Brody, would that be okay?" She watched his eyes light up.

"Yes, ma'am, that's not a problem. I was leaving anyway. I don't mind at all escorting this lovely little lady back to the hotel."

Jewel smiled at him and hooked her arm in his. As he led her away, she said, "So where are you from?"

Justin moved up behind her. "You're shameless."

She turned around and put her arm along Justin's shoulders, drawing him toward the raceway. "I know." Switching gears, she pointed at the track. "Tell me about this track. That damn car is still loose. God, I hate these short, tight tracks."

He pulled off his headset and looped it on his neck, then raised his sunglasses. For an instant, she forgot about the track.

Instead she drew in her breath, looking at his tanned face and his uncut hair blowing in the breeze. His expression serious, he rested his arm against hers. She felt the familiar sexual tension that stirred inside her every time she was close to him.

When she remembered the feel and power of his body under the clothes, she began to tingle all over. Corporate evening events, daytime training and corporate publicity activities had kept them so busy they fell into bed at night too tired to move. At one point they had flown to New York for a day to shoot a commercial, then flew back that evening. Cass had never known the mind-numbing fatigue she felt on this tour.

Out of consideration for her, most of the time Justin slept in his room because he needed to get up several hours earlier than she to set up the car or meet the crew. He didn't want to wake her. He knew she needed those few extra hours of sleep to stay healthy. She was constantly amazed at Justin's energy. Lately she was so tired she wondered if she was getting sick.

Cass watched him speak and remembered the most recent time they had been together. It had begun hot and fast, Justin out of control with desire. After his initial release, he recovered quickly and his lovemaking changed. His touch was gentle and loving. He worshiped her body, causing her to cry out with her need for him. Their third joining was so fulfilling it brought tears to her eyes.

When they were joined as one, everything in her world was balanced, as if she never needed to be anywhere else to be happy but in this man's arms.

She shook her head, trying to banish her desire. Later. It was time for business now, and she needed to concentrate on his words.

"Like your last race, the tight confines of this track are home to some of the closest fender-rubbing, tire-banging racing in the sport." He pointed at the tight curves. "We'll keep a close eye on Beau. He'll definitely try to take you out here. You're too close on points and if you miss a race, it'll give him the edge he needs."

She and Beau were running first and second in points, Beau in the lead. She nodded, acknowledging his advice, as Darrin walked up,

"Darrin, she says the car is still running loose. See if you can adjust the weight, maybe add a wedge. I don't want her breaking away on these curves tomorrow. The track is too tight for that."

Darrin nodded and left to assemble his crew.

Cass looked at the track and a rush of fear lashed through her. She shivered.

Justin turned his head toward her. "What's wrong?" He gave her a concerned, possessive look.

"I don't know. I don't get a warm, fuzzy feeling about this track." She watched the still practicing drivers' attempts to avoid contact at every turn.

"Babe, you'll be fine. You have a strong team supporting you, and you know I'll be right with you." He fingered the headset around his neck.

"Stay with me tonight, Justin, I need you." She'd never told him she needed him. Their mutual need was assumed but never voiced.

Another shiver sliced through her. Why did they never say the words aloud, she wondered.

"Are you sure, babe? You know I have to get up early and you haven't been getting enough sleep." He gently brushed his fingertip over the shadows below her eyes.

Tears formed in her eyes at the tenderness in his face. She couldn't voice what was wrong; she just had a bad feeling about tomorrow's race.

Justin frowned, watching the tears sparkle in her eyes. This was not a woman prone to fits of crying. The tears she produced when she raced were from stress, something Justin remembered doing himself. This was different. They made his stomach tense and drop to his knees, and a dark feeling started to take root in the back of his head.

"Damn." He looked around, seeing a spot between the trailers that appeared to be fairly secluded. He pulled her between them and wrapped her into his arms. He heard her sigh in relief, then he stepped back so no one could catch them embracing.

Damn, he hated this sneaking around. He slammed his frustration down. Cass needed his reassurance, not his anger.

"Cass, I'll stay with you tonight, gladly, you know that. It's only out of concern for you I'm not by your side every night. You understand, don't you?"

She nodded as he pulled out some tissues and began wiping away her tears, as if she were a precious child. "I know, Justin, I know. It's not that. I don't know what's wrong with me today." She tried to smile but the attempt was lost in her trembling lips.

"You're tired and stressed. These last two short tracks are some of the toughest NASCAR has to offer. You're doing fine, don't worry." He embraced her then, lightly kissing her lips. "I'm here for you, don't forget that," he said against her lips.

She hugged him tightly. "I know."

"I'll tell you what, let's go to dinner early tonight with your sister, then send her, Brody and Lee to Mrs. Kingsdale's pre-race event. You and I will be conveniently absent. Lee can make up an excuse. Then you and I…" he drew her closer, "…and the bed all night, how's that sound?"

She looked from side to side, as if checking to see whether anyone was walking by. Apparently satisfied, she placed her hand on his face and slowly moved it into his hair. With her other hand on the back of his head, she pulled his mouth to hers. Their kiss started out gentle but quickly exploded into passion.

Justin's arms came up to clasp her to him. There wasn't anything he wouldn't do for this woman.

Finally she pulled back. They both breathed hard, as if they'd run a mile. He noticed her tears had gone. He liked the cure he'd found.

"Sounds wonderful," she said, her voice husky, as she stepped back and out of his arms.

Putting his arm around her, he guided her back to the track. "Let's get out of here before we're caught."

They both spotted Darrin by the car, giving them the thumbs up.

"Now, go and earn your salary!" he commanded and fitted his headset back on.

She smiled and sauntered away.

~

That night Justin stayed with her while they sent a giddy Brody and Jewel off to the corporate dinner in their place. From the way Jewel and Brody kept looking at each other, he knew they were already smitten.

It was definitely a memorable evening of lovemaking. When Justin lingered over their morning-after kiss, he left no doubts that he would be sleeping with her from now on.

Chapter Eleven

Race Day

"Justin, God damn, she's still loose and I've got Beau right on my tail."

"Damn." She heard his response in the Com. Her hands jerked as Beau bumped her rear. She felt the back of the car break away from the track and turned her wheel to compensate, reclaiming her line.

"You've got eight laps to go," Justin said, "and I don't anticipate any more pits. You're in a good position. Ease off on the accelerator, you can afford to drop a few places if you need to. Beau's right behind you, leaving carnage in his wake. He's driven today. Be cautious."

Cass checked her rear view mirror and saw Beau behind her. This was a bad day. No adjustment they made seemed to compensate for the changing weather; the escalating heat was staggering. And the car had been loose all night, breaking away on almost every curve. It was a miracle she'd stayed in third position most of the day. The cars were packed like teens in a mosh pit. Probably the only reasons she'd maintained her position were that she'd started in third pole position and not much movement had occurred since the start of the race three hours earlier.

She watched Beau come up hard on her. "Justin," she warned.

Then she felt it. He struck her going into turn two, and the back of her car broke. This time it didn't stop, and there was nothing she could do to stop the spin she was about to take at one hundred and fifty miles per hour. She braced herself against the steering wheel and prayed. The mad spin seemed to happen in slow motion. She saw different angles of the track, feeling like she was floating. She smelled burning rubber and, although it seemed like hours, only seconds passed before the car crashed at the bottom of the track.

Cass looked around frantically. Justin was bellowing in her ear. Then a car struck the driver's side. She was jarred, her body straining. She grunted in pain and her body tried to jerk out of its harness. Her head struck the surrounding headrest, and something warm dripped down her face.

Then the car stilled.

Cass shook her head, her teeth gritted. If she was going to stay in the race, she needed to make some quick moves. Reaching over with her right hand, she punched the onboard camera, moving its line of sight off her. She depressed the clutch and jammed the car back into first gear. Sucking in a breath, she tried to calm her pounding heart. After a glance around to make sure the field had passed, she roared back onto the track behind the last car.

She was driving on instinct. She tried to raise her left arm, and a lightning bolt of pain ripped through her. She felt blood drip from her nose and down the right side of her face where she had struck the headrest. She tried to ignore it and focus on getting realigned during the caution.

"Cass, talk to me. I've got NASCAR officials asking me if you're okay."

"I think the car's a little worse for wear but how do I look?" she asked. She wasn't sure if she was on the track or not.

"You look good. I think that bent door will affect your aerodynamics, probably take a few mph off your speed. Other than that, you're holding your line. But your onboard camera is off line, so they can't see you," he told her matter-of-factly.

"Good, then tell them I'm okay to drive. The camera was knocked around some by the hit, no big deal."

"Okay."

She heard him talking to someone as she tried to get her bearings. Her nose was bleeding so much she couldn't get air through it. She started breathing through her mouth.

Nothing was going to stop her from finishing this race.

"Justin, where am I?"

"You're still in caution. Line up in third, that's where you were when they flagged the caution. Believe it or not, the lead car wrecked ahead of you, so you maintained your position. After the caution you'll have eight laps to complete."

Spotters began reading off the track conditions to her. She lined up. Her vision was a little fuzzy, and she shook her head, trying to work through the pain of her left arm. The cuts on her face were more of an annoyance than anything else. Her bleeding nose was the worst, because she couldn't breathe out of it. She clutched the steering wheel with her right hand. She got lined up but wasn't moving over the track to test her wheels. Justin recognized the fact immediately.

"Cass, your breathing's heavy. Are you sure you're all right?" he asked, suspicion in his voice.

She didn't answer as she concentrated on the green flag. Eight laps to go, she told herself, and on this track it would be quick. Beau was behind her. He had backed off now, probably realizing if he made her spin again he could be taking himself out as well. The green flag waved and they were back at full speed.

"Justin, I need to concentrate right now," she said, hoping that would shut him up, and it did. All she heard were spotters' reports of other racers' positions.

~

Four laps to go. She started panting. The pain in her arm was excruciating, causing her to groan. She gritted her teeth while she tried to maintain her position, weaving back and forth. Finally she allowed Beau to pass her and she eased back on the accelerator. She was still in fourth position and that wasn't a bad position to be in. Two more left, she thought, counting the seconds until the next lap. She felt the blood from her nose run down her neck.

Three laps.

Two.

One more.

She breathed a sigh of relief when she came up on the checkered flag.

"Justin, listen carefully," she instructed as she eased her foot off of the accelerator. "I'm taking the car to the repair area in the back. Keep the reporters away from the car and me. Don't let anyone but you come in contact with me. Tell them we want to look at the car damage immediately. Bring the other car around so I can move directly into it. Don't remove my helmet until we get into the car, and bring a towel with you."

"Shit, Cass, I don't like the sound of this."

"Do what I'm asking you or they'll pull me out of the Series. Do you understand what I'm telling you?" she yelled into the microphone.

"Yes." His voice was grim. "I understand."

She tried to slowly maneuver her way toward the back garage area.

"Cass, shut it down, we're going to push you. Lee's got the reporters handled."

She looked on each side and saw the pit crew surrounded the car, blocking her from anyone's view. She shut down the car and, with her right arm, she steered toward their repair area in the back. Once inside the garage, she let go of the wheel and sat back. The vision in her right eye was blocked with blood from the cut she assumed was on her forehead.

Justin's head appeared in the door after he removed the safety netting. "Can you get out?" he asked, as he started to remove her safety net. Then his voiced tensed with alarm. "Oh, my God, Cass, where's this blood coming from?" He frantically began to release the harness.

"It's from my nose, not a big deal, don't worry about it. I think it's my left arm we need to be worried about because it's not functioning very well."

Justin swore. He tried to extract her from the cockpit and she cried out in pain.

"I've got to remove your helmet."

"Fine, are all the press and NASCAR officials gone?" she asked anxiously. "If they see me now, you know they'll bench me for the next race." Panic was at the edge of her consciousness.

"I'm not so sure that's a bad idea at this point. What the hell were you thinking?" He finally removed her helmet. Looking at her face, he cursed even more.

"I think it's just a cut on my forehead and my nose is bleeding. It's a lot of blood. It's my arm I'm worried about."

"Okay, okay. Here, move your body around in the seat so I can pull you out. This is going to hurt."

He put his hands under both of her arms and hauled her partway out of the car. Pain blinding her, she cried out. He released her and came around her right side. "Put your good hand around my neck."

She followed his orders. He put his strong arm around her body and tugged her out of the car. He swung her fully into his arms and carried her to the waiting vehicle.

"Justin, have Brody bring Jewel to the hotel to meet us," Cass ordered.

He laid her gently in the back seat and turned to Darrin. "Tell Lee it's all clear, and clean up the blood in the driver seat before NASCAR inspects the car. I'll see Lee at the hotel. Get Brody and tell him to bring Jewel."

Justin slid into the car with a towel in his hand. He instructed the driver to return to the hotel. Shifting Cass onto his lap, he told her to lean back her head. When she did, he applied the small towel to her nose. He took another towel and carefully wiped her face and neck, then pressed it against the cut on her forehead.

"Is it broken?" he asked.

She assumed he was talking about her arm. "I think it's dislocated. When we get back to the hotel, Jewel can take care of it. It's happened before." She laughed shakily. "You don't think I've lived the life I have without ever incurring any injuries, do you?" She smiled, but he wasn't smiling back. Instead, he looked ready to explode.

A muscle in his cheek clenched as he wiped the blood off of her face. She stopped the movement of his hand with hers.

"Justin, I'm not injured that bad. I'll be fine. It's a head wound, so it's bleeding a lot, okay?" She rubbed her thumb over his hand.

He leaned his forehead against hers. "I don't like your blood on my hands," he said simply.

Cass closed her eyes. The minute she did, she relived the crash, feeling the jolt, fear choking her, her heart slamming in her chest as if it were happening all over again. She opened her eyes, hoping the memory would disappear.

Justin's forehead still rested against hers, his dark head so close she could touch it. Unable to resist, she reached out and rested her hand on his head, saying a quick thank you that the accident hadn't been worse. He tightened his arms around her. The drive to the hotel took only a few more minutes. The driver dropped them at the back, and they entered from one of the side entrances, bypassing the lobby. Justin carried her to her room and laid her on the bed.

Justin left to search for a first aid kit. Grunting with pain, Cass peeled out of her blood-splattered racing suit. Then she gritted her teeth and eased her way into the bathroom to wash off the blood. She washed most of it off when Jewel and Brody came crashing into the hotel room. A moment later, Justin arrived with a first aid kit.

Jewel settled Cass onto the bed, and she and Justin patched up the cuts on her face. Her nose had finally stopped bleeding, the shock wearing off. Loss of blood and shock from the accident combined to make her woozy, the room starting to tilt.

"Uh oh, big sister, you've lost all of your color."

"Jewel, take care of my arm. You know how it's done."

Jewel chuckled. "I remember. Do you?"

Cass returned her sarcastic laugh.

Justin looked at the two of them as if they'd lost their minds. Jewel glanced around, obviously searching for something. Justin stepped up, and Jewel nodded at him.

"That would be great. Get up on the bed behind her and brace her from the rear."

Not questioning her authority, he toed off his shoes and crawled up on the bed. Gently lifting Cass, he eased behind her, then pulled her between his legs, his back resting against the headboard. Jewel reached over and positioned his arms, one wrapped around Cass' right shoulder and the other around her waist.

Justin leaned forward and whispered into Cass' ear, "This wasn't really what I was thinking as far as getting you between my legs, babe."

She laughed at his attempt to lighten the mood. But the slight movement hurt and her laugh turned into a wince.

"Okay, you guys, we're ready. Cass, you know how this goes. Justin, hold on tight." Jewel raised Cass' arm and Justin tightened his hold on her body. Jewel made eye contact with Cass. "Ready?"

Cass nodded.

"Okay, one, two..." Bracing her leg on the bed, she jerked Cass' arm straight out. Cass attempted to arch out of Justin's arms, but he held tight. As the pain of her shoulder snapping into place radiated though her body, she howled louder than a pack of wolves on a full moon night.

Cass slammed her head back against Justin's chest, closing her eyes and gritting her teeth. Jewel slowly lowered her arms, and gently probed Cass' shoulder with her fingertips.

"That did it. It'll be sore for several days."

Peeling her eyelids open, Cass watched Jewel grab an ace bandage from the first aid kit. With Justin's help, she lifted

Cass and wrapped her arm to her body. The pain knifing through Cass' shoulder and arm lowered to a dull ache.

"Here, these will help you sleep tonight." Jewel pulled something from her purse. "Tylenol with Codeine. I never leave home without them." She smiled while Brody handed her a glass of water for Cass. "Thanks, hon," she said to Brody.

Cass saw Justin raise his eyebrows at Brody, who gave them both a *what* look. Cass downed the pills, and leaned back against Justin.

"Now you, big sister, are going to get some much needed rest." Jewel signaled for Justin to join her by the door. He gently eased his body from behind Cass. Repositioning the pillow, he laid her head on it, and crossed to the door.

"Justin, she looks exhausted. I'm concerned about her." Familiar ice blue eyes pinned him down.

He raised his hands. "There's nothing I can do to slow her down." He gazed at Cass, sleeping on the bed, looking beautiful even with her mouth open and snoring softly. His heart twisted inside him. She'd come so close to being hurt seriously today. "She's a stubborn woman."

Jewel laid her hand on his arm. "I know, but can you get her to rest for a few days? Physically she wasn't injured badly, but that shoulder has always given her problems. And her fatigue will slow the healing process. Tell her Brody's taking me to the beach for few days, so she won't worry about entertaining me. And keep her in bed, okay?"

Brody draped his arm around Jewel's shoulders.

Justin looked at the two of them and saw their mutual affection for each other. "Okay." He frowned at the handsome race car driver. "Brody," Justin said, a warning in his voice.

Brody nudged Jewel toward the door, telling her he would meet her downstairs. He turned toward Justin and held up his hands, as if in surrender.

"I know what you're going to say. All I can say in defense is, in the short time I've known Jewel, she stirs me like no other woman. I think I'm hopelessly in love with her." His hands dropped to his sides.

Justin clapped his hand on Brody's shoulder. "Believe me, I know these women can cast a spell on a man. Be responsible and protect her, for Cass and for me—and most of all for her," he said, feeling paternal. He was nine years older than Brody, and felt more like his father right now than his boss.

Brody grinned. "I will, don't worry. Take care of Cass."

Justin released Brody's shoulder, nodding. As Brody left the room, Justin leaned over Cass, watching her chest expand and contract with each breath. He crouched down and pushed the blond locks from her bandaged forehead. When he'd seen her car spinning around, unable to do anything to stop it, he'd not been able to breathe. Inside his head a primal scream had started. His fists had bunched at his side, and if Beau had been within reach, he would have forgotten about racing protocol and ripped his ugly head off his neck.

In that second, he knew he loved her. If she died, a part of him would die too.

He shook his head now in wonder. *I love her. I love her more than life itself.*

She stirred and slowly opened her eyes. "Justin, come to bed," she said sleepily.

He smiled, knowing she was acting on instinct. It warmed him that she thought of him even in her drugged state. He rested a hand on her cheek and she closed her eyes again. Her uninjured hand crept up to capture his. He shook his head in wonder.

What a woman I have chosen to love.

A woman who would almost kill herself to win a race—passionate in her attempt to accomplish what no woman had. He eased her hand from his. He stripped and slipped into the bed, pulling the blankets over both of them. Then he carefully wrapped his arms around her. In her sleep, she turned and wiggled against him to get closer.

He felt the familiar quickening of his heart. Putting his lips against her forehead, he kissed her gently. She sighed in her sleep. He closed his eyes, the stress of the day and the fatigue of the tour lessening, his body relaxing. With Cass safely in his arms, he fell into a blissful sleep.

Sometime in the night Cass awoke, thrashing and crying out his name. He quieted her, kissing her, stroking her, finally wrapping her back into his arms. He remembered the nightmares well.

~

Justin experienced an erotic dream so vivid it seemed real. Arching, he pushed against warm wetness lubricating his manhood. "Ahhh," he said. Hearing his voice, the remnants of sleep dissipated. He became aware of his dick, rock hard and straining upward. Cracking his eyes open, he saw Cass' golden hair strewn over his body as she sucked him awake, his hand buried in her hair. From the curtained window, early morning rays of sun formed a halo around her hair, as if she were a naughty angel.

He moaned as she wrapped her tongue around the head of his cock, and with the most gratifying movement, she pulled his penis inside her mouth and gently sucked. "Cass," he said, pulling her head up.

She slid upward, running kisses up his belly, his chest. Her lips blazed the way, leaving a fire where they passed, finally coming to rest on his mouth. His tongue mated with hers, his hand burying in the back of her hair. He was ready to take her, ride her. He wanted to be inside her.

"You..." he panted as her hand slid up and down his chest, "...are supposed..." he groaned as she impaled her wet vagina on his dick, "...to be resting."

He grunted, dropping his hands to her hips. She leaned forward and silenced him with another deep passionate kiss, her lips moving from his mouth, wetting it, and running down his neck. He ran his hands up her back, encouraging her to thrust with him, reminding himself to avoid her bandaged arm.

Sliding her legs under her, she rocked against him. In response, he bucked his hips, his balls drawing up.

"Cass," he groaned, as she braced her hands against his muscled chest.

She bent her good arm. Between long, slow moves, she kissed him, moaning his name against his lips.

She is so damn sexy.

She moved forward and back, her hips rolling, sliding over his dick. Her breath sucked in. Leaning over him, she lengthened her moves. Justin tensed, on the edge of coming.

"Justin, come with me," she breathed against his ear. She rocked faster, her body moving in symmetry with his. Leaning back, she arched at the same instant Justin cried out with explosive pleasure and sweet release. He clutched her hips flush against his as he thrust as deep into her as he could go. Then he convulsed beneath her, his harsh breaths filling the corners of the hotel room. Heaven had never felt so good.

Trembling with her own release, she eased forward to rest her glistening body on his. He ran his hands down her back, enjoying the feel of her slight body resting against his chest. He had no words to describe the pleasure he felt. Any emotion he tried to express would be inadequate, so he just held her, and stroked her. Her breathing became low and soft against his neck. He gently eased her to his side, keeping her locked in his arms. He brushed the hair away from her face. She opened her eyes and smiled.

She was lovely, he thought, her beauty going beyond the physical. She was pure in heart as well as in her soul. Her energy for life—embracing the risks the way she did—sometimes left him breathless.

"Cass, when you spun around the track last night…" He paused and swallowed his emotions. He'd tried so hard to deny his fear but this time he couldn't. Cass stroked his cheek. "I was so deathly scared, so scared," he repeated. "It was at that moment I realized how much I love you, and how I hadn't told you. I was so scared of losing you, I… do you understand what I'm trying to tell you?" He stopped because he simply ran out of words.

"Oh, Justin." A sob tore from her throat. "I love you too, more than you will ever know, more than I can express."

Justin cupped her cheek and kissed her. "I love you," he said against her lips. Between tender kisses on lips, he said the three most precious words over and over, never wanting to stop.

She smiled at him, kissing him back.

Finally, he placed his forehead against hers. "Marry me, Cass. Share my life. Have my children. Pledge yourself to me and me only." He pulled back to see her response.

Her features softened and tears formed in her eyes. "Oh, Justin."

He laughed, scooting closer to her. "Is that 'Oh, Justin, yes,' or 'Oh, Justin, what a fool you are'?"

"No."

Justin tried to stay calm, but his stomach felt as if it slammed to the floor.

"No," she said again, her voice ragged. "I don't mean *no* ... I mean, no, you're not a fool. You must know I would marry you in a minute, tomorrow, hell, today. But we can't."

"The tour and Mrs. Kingsdale?" Justin swore.

"Do you really need to ask?"

Justin huffed out a breath and flipped over on his back, "I told you, I won't let her run my life. Are you sure you're saying no because of that, or is that an excuse? Maybe you don't really want to marry me?" He struck out at her like an angry child. He knew he was acting like a jerk and hated himself for it. Looking at Cass' stunned expression, he shook his head in self-disgust.

"Justin, how can you say that? You know that's not true."

He laid an arm over his eyes to block out her accusing stare. "I know." He lay there for a moment to absorb her rejection. He tried to tell himself it was the tour, it was Mrs. Kingsdale and all the events going on in their life. But a small part of him wondered if she really didn't want him. Her hand rested on his chest, and he took a deep breath, trying to swallow his disappointment.

I can't do this.

Justin drew in another breath and gently removed her hand. He flipped the blanket from his side of the bed, reaching for his pants. Not glancing at her, he dressed.

"Justin?"

He pulled on his shoes. Sitting on the edge of the bed, he lowered his head into his hands in a gesture of defeat.

She moved behind him and laid her head on his shoulder. "Talk to me, please. Understand that I do love you, and this has nothing to do with us."

Something dampened his shirt, and he knew it was tears running down her cheeks. He straightened and looked over his shoulder at her golden head resting against his shoulder. Even now he wanted her. Even with the annoyance and the hurt tearing through his guts.

"Doesn't it?" he asked, his brow furrowed with hurt.

She jerked as if someone shot her. He almost took back his words but he couldn't.

Instead, he stood, extricating himself from her alluring touch. She dropped onto her back. Seeing her unhappy expression, he knelt next to the bed, facing her. He ran his hands over her sore shoulder and watched her wince. In an attempt to change the subject, he said, "Still hurt a lot?"

She shook her head. "It's not anywhere near as painful as it was last night."

He nodded and leaned over to grab the bottle of Tylenol with Codeine that Jewel had left. He gave her two pills and the glass of water on the nightstand, warm from standing out all night.

"Here, take these."

"I hate them. They knock me out."

"I don't care." His voice came out rougher than he'd planned.

Her surprised expression met his.

Sighing, he softened his voice and guided her hand to her mouth. "Take them. You need the rest and it will help the swelling."

She placed them in her mouth, then washed them down and handed him back the glass.

He traced his fingertips lightly down her cheek, then stood, shoving his hands in his pockets. "I'm going to take a walk, get us something to eat. I'll be back in a little while."

I need to get out.

"Please don't leave like this," she pleaded. "We need to discuss this."

"What's to discuss? I want to get married. I want us to commit to each other, to have children together. I want forever, you don't."

"It's not that simple!" Cass cried out.

"No, Cass!" Justin yelled, his emotions bubbling to the surface. "It *is* that easy! This tour and this sponsor obviously mean more to you than I do."

Clutching the blankets above her breasts, she sat up. He watched angry flags of color stain her cheeks and the fight brewing in her eyes.

"Justin, that isn't true and you know it. I don't know why you are saying these things, I don't understand."

He threw up his hands and walked to the door.

"Justin, don't."

He stopped at her low voice, remembering a time when he'd used the same word to stop her from leaving.

He didn't turn around. He knew his emotions were out of control. "I need to go. Don't ask me to stay. I'm afraid I'll say something else that I'll regret."

She choked, as if she were swallowing a cry.

"I'll be back later," he said, then quietly closed the door.

Chapter Twelve

Cass lay back in the bed, tears coursing down her face.

She feared this would happen. He was beyond stubborn. She threw one of the pillows at the door. He wanted his own way or no way at all. The man who stomped out of the room reminded her of the angry person she had first met. She'd thought she was taming him, but he apparently thought the same thing about her.

Sniffing, Cass raised her chin. He wasn't going to have it all his way. She was going to finish this tour and she was going to meet her sponsor's expectations. Unless it killed her, neither Justin nor anyone else was going to stop her. Without thinking, she rolled over on her bad arm and yelped like a hurt puppy. Then she laughed hollowly.

Being killed was a distinct possibility.

Thoughts of Justin made her smile wilt and die. She loved him so much, far surpassing any emotion she'd ever experienced before. She wanted to share everything he wanted, but she also wanted to fulfill her dream. Just this once she didn't want to be the one to give up her dream in the name of love and responsibilities. She had told herself she didn't resent giving up her career to raise Jewel. She'd lied. Marriage, kids, they didn't fit in the picture right now. She wasn't going to give up racing again. Not when the cup was so close, she could almost feel it in her hands.

Tears fell harder when she thought of the possible consequences this path had for her.

I can't lose him.

Jewel's pills finally took their intended effect. Her last thought was of Justin and how much she loved him.

Justin sat in the room next to Cass', deep in thought. He had walked for several hours, found a grocery store and gotten some food, then returned to his hotel room to brood. He had acted as childishly as when they first met, using rage and anger to push her away. He berated himself, but couldn't bring himself to go to her room and apologize. He had wanted to push her away, to keep away the pain of any possible loss. The world thought he was tough, but deep down he was scared, terrified.

He wanted her to stop racing. He wanted her to tell him he was more important than this crazy tour. With every race, he relived his accident. Every time she drove, he projected his fears that what happened to him might happen to her. How could he change when he knew his fears could so easily become reality?

If he couldn't have all of her—one hundred percent commitment—then he didn't want anything at all. He didn't want to be her convenient tour lover; he wanted to spend the rest of his life as her partner. He smiled when he thought about the first time they had met and he pulled her into the dirt. She had come up fighting, like the strong woman she was. He was sure she wasn't going to take his rejection lying down.

He made a difficult decision: he wasn't going to sleep with her again until he had a commitment from her. He wasn't going to be her clandestine lover. His jaw firmed when he thought about her reaction. Grabbing the sandwich he had brought for her, he opened the connecting door and stepped into her room.

The pacing woman who greeted him had him gritting his teeth.

"Where have you been?" she demanded.

He dropped the bag onto her table and casually sat in the cushioned chair. "Out," he said.

"That's it? Just *out*? You've been gone," she looked at her watch, "seven hours. I was getting worried."

He shrugged, trying to look indifferent.

Her hands curled into fists. She looked as if she were about to breathe fire.

God, she's beautiful when she's angry.

"You know, Cass, you're already starting to sound like my wife. Are you sure you don't want to take on the role?" A smile quirked the corners of his lips.

She grabbed a stray pillow off the bed and threw it at him, then winced and cradled her arm.

He caught the pillow, then dropped in on the chair and approached her. He put his arm around her and pulled her to the bed, forcing her to sit on the mattress edge.

"Calm down, you're going to hurt yourself." He released her and dropped back down onto the chair.

She glared at him. "This attitude isn't appealing to me. What the hell's the matter with you?"

"What's the matter with me?" His anger rose out of the calmness he'd tried so hard to maintain. One miserable minute. That's all it had taken for her to break down his barriers.

He moved right into her face. "What's the matter is I'm angry." He bit off the words. "I'm not going to be your convenient lover. I want more between us. If you're not willing to give it, then I think we need to cool off this little affair."

Her nostrils flared in outrage. "Cool off? What are you talking about? Seven hours ago we pledged our love to each other. What's to cool off? All I said was I didn't want to get married right now. I want to finish the tour and meet my responsibilities. Is it too much to ask you to wait six months? Because if it is, maybe you're not the man I thought you were."

Justin felt like he carried a keg of dynamite inside him and every word she said was a lit match.

"I gave up my career to raise Jewel," she continued. "I'm not saying I regret it for a minute, but now I have another chance to make my dream come true. Am I a bad person to want that to happen?"

"But at what price?" he asked in a gritty voice. He waved his hand at her arm. "Maybe your life, maybe me." He was testing her, he knew, but he needed to hear what she would say.

"I don't think you're being reasonable," she argued.

"What price, Cass?" he yelled. "I watched you spin out yesterday in the middle of forty cars going 150 miles per hour. What price are you willing to pay?"

"Is that what this is about? Yesterday's crash? You know that happens every day in this business. You know how safe those cars are, and you know it's nearly impossible to be seriously injured…" She stopped suddenly, as if realizing what she had said.

His eyes scanned her face. "Is it?" He saw tears well in her eyes. His voice gentling, he asked again, "What price, Cass?" He wanted to pull her into his arms and confess his love over and over. He wanted to tell her he would support her, no matter what. But he needed her to examine her profession and see how much she was sacrificing to achieve her dream.

Her shoulders slumped. She shook her head defeated, as if she knew there was nothing she could say in her defense. Then, like a fighter, her chin lifted. "What does *cool off* mean?"

Justin sighed. "I've already told you I'm not going to be your convenient lover. I think I should probably stay in my room for now on." He pushed the bag of food around the table.

He heard Cass suck in a breath then exhale it slowly. She got up from the bed and walked to the window. Her back to him, she looked out. He watched her, hoping he was going to hear the right answer.

He had just asked her to choose between her career and him.

Shifting in the chair, he waited. She remained motionless by the window. He steepled his fingers under his chin. Finally, he blurted out, "Cass, you're being childish. Talk to me."

She crossed her arms over her chest. "I will say this once and once only." She continued to look out the window. "Your ultimatum does not deserve an answer."

Justin stepped up to her. She deliberately turned her head and glared at him. He saw the determination in her stare. And in that moment, in his mind, he knew her choice. His eyes memorized her face, moving over the classic lines, falling to her lips remembering their lovemaking. He wanted to tug her into his arms and draw those luscious lips into his. His gaze lifting, he watched her eyes narrow, as if she knew what he thought and didn't like it.

He stepped back, threw up his hands and left the room. *Screw it.*

~

He felt Cass' reckless rage and anger every time she strapped into a car. He realized it was what drove her to win in the next five consecutive races. Her furious driving style and their strained relationship sent Justin further into disillusionment of her so-called love for him. Their publicity appearances were clearly strained; their one-on-one interactions even more so. Mrs. K called him to warn them to look more amiable with each other. When he relayed the message to Cass, she gave him a *screw off* look and continued walking.

Chapter Thirteen

Race 16
Dover Downs International Speedway
Dover, Delaware

    Cass pulled into the pits following her victory lap to be greeted by a scowling Justin and an ecstatic crew. After sixteen races she was finally leading the tour, twenty points ahead of Beau, who was running second. She stopped at victory row, her car surrounded by a swarm of people.
    Beau drove by. Pointing, he yelled, "Watch your back, sweet cheeks." He gave a catcall whistle.
    For a minute, she sat in the car and leaned her head back, helmet and all. She let the familiar vertigo pass that she had been getting at the finish of each race. It was the same swirling feeling she'd been getting each morning. This morning it had sent her running to the toilet to seek relief.
    Suddenly, Justin was there, releasing her harness, helping her take off her helmet, lecturing her as usual for the damage on the car from the last hit she gave to Beau. She hadn't let him

help her out of the car for eight weeks, but today she didn't have the energy to fight him. She laid her helmet down next to her and leaned on him as she shimmied out of the car.

He looked down at her. Concern flickered in his eyes, and he stopped yelling at her.

What a change. She sighed in relief. Someone shoved a sponsor's hat at Justin, and he flipped it on Cass's head. Cass answered the reporters' questions, smiling, trying to maintain her professional demeanor, but she thought even the worst critic wouldn't buy her act. She glanced at Justin, who was heading off reporters.

Cass knew how she looked: dark circles under her eyes, her complexion tinged with gray, slumping shoulders and neck, as if her head was too heavy to lift. She didn't have the spirit to respond any more to Justin's needling. All they'd been doing lately was snarl at each other.

"Cass, your car took a pretty big hit from Beau," a reporter asked. "Will you be ready for the next race?"

Lifting a weak hand, she pointed at Justin. "That's the man to ask. Now, if you'll excuse me."

She slipped her arm from Justin's and slowly made her way to the bathroom, leaving him swarmed by reporters and unable to follow her. She didn't turn back. For the first time since the beginning of the tour, she wondered if she was going to make it.

~

Cass clung to Justin's arm as they made their way around the room of the Blair Hotel in their obligatory evening publicity event in honor of her win. She tripped over the hem of her gown. He turned toward her, his eyes narrowed.

"Are you okay?"

"Honestly?" She clutched his arm tighter. "I think something I ate isn't agreeing with me. I feel positively green."

He pulled her to the wall and frowned at her. "You've been green for several weeks now. When are you going to admit you're not feeling well?"

Cass almost felt relief when she spotted Mrs. K walking toward them on the arm of one of her investors. The cosmetic tycoon unhitched her arm, giving the man a royal smile that wiped away when she turned toward Cass and Justin. As she neared them, her features seemed to sharpen, reminding Cass of Cruella DeVille.

"Mr. Steed, I expect that you will get this woman to a doctor as soon as possible. I don't need my most popular commodity looking like death warmed over." It was a queen's command, one that didn't brook any argument—from either of them.

"Mrs. K, I'm fine, a little tired. I don't think a doctor is necessary." Cass' flow of words stopped when Mrs. K gave her a *my commands will not be questioned* look.

"I agree," Justin said.

Cass pursed her lips in frustration. She turned around to look for an escape route from her two wardens. Apparently, she turned too quickly because suddenly she felt dizzy, the room tilting. Her knees buckled and her world went black. She felt herself falling but couldn't do anything to stop it.

~

Cass was warm and secure for the first time in a long time. A cool cloth draped over her forehead. Slowly her eyes opened. Her first sight was Justin's worried face. She smiled at his scowl.

"Welcome back." He straightened the cloth on her forehead. He was perched on the side of the bed, still in his formal attire. His jacket and necktie had been removed, his crisp white shirt unbuttoned. He looked handsome as usual. A lock of his black hair fell into his eyes. Cass reached up and brushed it back into place.

"Cass, you're going to the doctor tomorrow if I have to take you myself, and that's the end of this discussion."

She sighed, dropping her hand. "Fine," she said, attempting to rise.

His strong hands pressed against her shoulders, pushing her back down.

"What is it with you? Don't you know when to stay down? You continue to walk into the punches," he said, frustration in his voice.

"I said I would go. Don't you have someone else to harass?" She rolled away from him, curling up her legs. She reached up her hand to adjust the cloth on her forehead. She heard Justin sigh, then felt his hand stroke down her back. It was the first time in weeks he had touched her with a hint of his old tenderness.

"Cass, I..." His voice caught.

Curious, she twisted around to look at him. His eyes had softened from their usual frustration.

"I worry about you." He ran the back of his hand over her cheek.

Cass wrapped his hand in hers, pressing it against her cheek. She closed her eyes, reveling in the pleasure of his touch. It seemed so long since the fight two months ago when their beautiful lovemaking had gone so wrong. When they had said things that Cass wasn't sure they could take back. But one thing she did know: she loved this man so much it hurt. There were times like now when she questioned why she even considered giving up his love for the track.

Opening her eyes, she stared into his. "Justin, I love you so much." She moved his hand from her to cover her heart, where it hurt from the thought of losing him. Her heart began thumping wildly where his hand lay. Even the thought of his touch sent her into a wild wanting.

"Feel what you do to me." Her need was mirrored by the spark in his. His fingers moved, and he caressed her breast. She blew out a breath and closed her eyes. His arms slid around her body and he lifted her against him. His groan matched her sigh.

"I don't know what happened between us, but I want to make it right." She pulled back slightly, and her eyes roamed over his face. "I don't care any more. I can't do this without you, without us. I give up. I'll stop racing if that's what you want."

"Ah, babe," he said, placing a gentle kiss on her brow. Then he pulled her into the warmth of his embrace.

"No, Cass, I was being selfish, projecting my fears onto you. I don't want you to stop, I know how much this means to you." His leaned back, framing her face with his hands. His thumbs rubbed the tears from her face. "I don't know what got into me. I think I was scared. I love you too." His voice broke and his lips moved forward to claim hers.

Cass felt the wetness on his face mingling with her own tears. Her love deepened for this man who claimed he was never gentle. She reached up and began to remove his shirt. As if coming to his senses, he laid his hands over hers.

"You're not feeling well. Are you sure you're up to this? Because once you touch me, I won't be able to stop."

"I love you and I want to feel you inside me," she whispered.

He let out an audible breath and released her hands. Cass made quick work of undressing him, no lingering over foreplay. She needed him. Her hurried movements reflected her need. She was scared something would suddenly change. He eased down next to her on the bed, running his hand along her ribs and over her hips to curve on her rear. He pulled her close to rest her core against his hard penis.

There is nothing better then being naked with this man.

"Feel what you do to me," he said, and growled against her lips before claiming them. His tongue swept along the seam of her lips and thrust forward into her mouth. She ran her hands along his muscular body. Groaning at her touch, he rolled her over and entered her in one movement. She gasped in pleasure. He pushed forward, filling her so completely it staggered her. He took her lips, his body driving in rhythm with hers.

"Cass, Cass. God, how I love you," he chanted, plunging full length into her.

She wrapped her feet around his ass, running her toes over him. He answered with a moan, his neck arching, his body tensed. He drove faster, in and out with his hard cock.

"Come with me," he panted against her neck, his thrusts growing longer and harder.

It was Cass' turn to groan, her heart accelerating. The familiar tightness began in her vagina and radiated over her entire body. She arched into him, crying out as he did the same. He crushed her to him and held her, pulsating, spilling himself so fully she felt his cum trickling down the inside of her thighs.

Sighing, she ran her hands up the sides of his neck, burying them in his hair. He sagged on top of her, breathing heavily. After a moment, he lifted his head and kissed her. His mouth lingered against hers. She felt him smile as he grew rock hard inside of her.

"Now, what was it we were fighting about?" he asked, grinning.

Her smile matched his. "It doesn't matter. All that matters is we stick together."

He laughed, sliding his penis inside and out until she gasped.

"We are together, babe, and that's how I intend to stay."

Chapter Fourteen

"Ms. Jamison, good afternoon. I'm Dr. Jessup, and very much a fan, I might add." The doctor's large hand swallowed Cass'. "Tell me what seems to be the problem," he said, planting himself in the tall, rolling physician's chair that placed him at eye level as she sat on the exam table, her jean-covered legs dangling.

"I've not been feeling well for about three weeks. I don't know, maybe the flu. I'm having a hard time holding down food, dizzy spells." Cass flipped her hand in a dismissing gesture. "Stuff like that."

"Hmm." The gray-haired doctor did a standard check up, asking her to breathe deeply, examining her ears and eyes, probing her abdominal area. After fifteen minutes of questions, he sat back in the chair and said, "Hmm."

"What is it, Doctor?"

"You seem fine, you're not showing any signs of flu or anything else. Your lungs are clear. Your throat looks good. No signs that you are seriously ill." He rose and moved over to a tall cabinet. "I suspect you're experiencing nothing more complicated than exhaustion. How have your menstrual cycles been?"

Cass thought back to her last period. It was over four weeks ago, maybe longer. "I haven't had one yet this month, but I've faithfully taken my pills."

He nodded, coming toward her with a small bottle in his hand. "Don't get too worried. It's not uncommon for women who are under extreme physical stress to decrease menstrual activity. Some don't have periods at all. I'm going to have you give a blood and urine sample. I suspect you might be anemic. This is a sample of vitamins that are high in iron. I'll write a prescription for something to settle your stomach, so you can hold down food." He pointed a finger at her in an accusatory manner. "You need to get some rest, young lady." He handed her the vitamins, then scribbled the prescription.

"Doctor, you're not going to pull me from driving, are you?"

Dr. Jessup handed her the prescription. "No, you can drive. You're young and you'll recover quickly with these vitamins. This is a message from your body telling you to slow down a little." He smiled at her sigh of relief. "I'll send my nurse in to collect those samples and we'll call you in a few days with the results."

"Thank you, Doctor," Cass said, relieved there was nothing seriously wrong.

"And, Cass?" he said, looking at her with his hand on the door.

"Yes, Doctor?" She jumped off the table in search of her clothes.

"You go get them on the track. You're the best thing that's happen to that sport in forty years." He gave her a thumbs up, then left the room.

Justin threw down the magazine. He had been trying to read, but it was useless. He got up and began to pace around the waiting room. The other waiting room occupants looked at him in irritation. God, this waiting was killing him. He had literally kidnapped Cass and sat her into the car to get her to the doctor's this morning. Glancing at the TV, he saw a picture of Cass on the screen. He moved forward and turned up the volume.

"Well, folks, big news in sports this week. The breathtaking Cass Jamison takes another Nextel NASCAR race, maintaining the lead on points and definitely a contender for the famed NASCAR Nextel Cup, which, by the way, has never been won by a woman." They showed a picture of her, very pale and shaky, allowing Justin to pull her out of the car. Cass' arm remained hooked through his as they walked through the crowd.

It was clear she wasn't well. She was swaying on her feet, and Justin's concern showed on his face for the whole world to see. Her hand was around his neck as he talked to her. As much as they had been fighting, as much as they tried to hide their attraction, it was there for everyone to see. It was there when his hand touched the small of her back, holding her upright, it was there when they leaned toward each other. It was a familiarity that wasn't usually found between crew chief and driver. Normally they tried to hide it, but at that moment, Justin's concern for her state of health had overridden his caution.

"It's clear we aren't the only one concerned about the golden beauty, as you can see here." Another picture flashed on the screen. It was Justin and Cass at the Martinsville Speedway, when he had been showing her the track. Her hand rested on his shoulder and she leaned into him when he talked. Although he was absorbed in pointing out the curves, she had turned to him, trying to hear him. In one unguarded moment, the look she gave him was clearly more than *just friends*. It was a look of wanting, of desire, of love. As her hand moved to stroke the hair below his collar, she moved closer and said something into his ear that made his eyes widen in surprise. He smiled straight into her eyes before they both turned to look at the track again.

Justin sighed. Their mission to keep their relationship a secret was a failure. He remembered that moment well—it was right before he had hauled her behind the trailers and kissed her for all he was worth.

"Although these two deny any deeper relationship than crew chief and driver, we wonder if they realize we're not as stupid as we look." The reporter flashed to the moment when he'd asked them about their relationship and Cass had bawled the press out. Justin remembered her words. He had been so proud of her, standing up to them.

"Yes, folks, I think Justin Steed has finally met his match with this driver." Another picture flashed of Justin and Cass arguing, faces close, breath mingled, then Justin stepped back and threw up his hands and walked off. The camera turned to Cass, showing something he hadn't seen, the anguish crossing Cass' face, the disappointment as tears glistened in her eyes. Then she shook her head and walked in the other direction.

The reporter and his photographer had caught them after the Bristol Motor Speedway race when Justin was giving her a hard time about banging up the car. She'd yelled at him to drive the car himself if he didn't like the way she did it.

Looking at the TV screen, Justin ran a hand through his hair in frustration, asking himself what he had almost thrown away in the name of his pride and fear. Telling her it was because she wasn't willing to sacrifice her career for him. But in his heart he knew he had struck out because he was scared the same thing that happened to him would happen to her. He knew the odds were against it, but he couldn't help the way he felt every time he put her into that car.

"All issues aside," the reporter said, "this station is as concerned as the rest of the world with the news that Cass Jamison collapsed yesterday at a corporate sponsor party. We hope all is well, Cass." He put aside the piece of paper and faced the camera directly. "And on a personal note, all of us here at the station want to send a message to these obvious lovers in denial. It's okay, guys, we all support you. I don't think you need to hide anymore." They flashed to a picture of Justin helping Cass out of the car, and cradling her in his arms. The crew surrounded her as he swung her around. Her head was thrown back and she was laughing. He was laughing with her, both staring at each other with obvious, deep affection.

Justin shook his head. It had been her first win, they had been so happy. Justin turned his head when a hand clasped his. Cass moved next to him, watching the TV. He squeezed her hand.

"With eighteen races to go in the tour, we'll be waiting for the word that a healthy Cass Jamison will join us for the next race in two weeks. We're all pulling for this incredible female to take this tour. Good luck, Cass," he said, smiling. "That's it for sports tonight, folks. We leave you with a few pictures of the NASCAR action."

The credits started rolling as they flashed pictures of Cass' car banging against Beau's as she roared past him on the inside, pushing him toward the wall. Then they flashed to her sitting on top of the car, waiting for the word that the race had been canceled, a steady rain soaking her hair. Her face was turned up toward the sky, her mouth opened as if to catch rain, and she looked stunning. With a switch, the TV flashed to her wreck, her car sailing around in circles, coming to rest in the median. Another car zoomed up and crashed into her side. Then the last picture was Cass and Justin smiling at each other, holding up a trophy for the Darlington race she had won. As champagne sprayed over them, they both laughed, joy in their expressions, obviously madly in love.

Cass laughed now at the TV screen, then the scenes ended, cutting to a coffee commercial. Justin stood for a moment as Cass' hand entwined with his. Then the consequences of the report hit him.

"I guess we failed pretty miserably at hiding our relationship." He waved his hand toward the TV.

Cass laughed and hugged him to her side. "Who cares?"

"Unfortunately, Mrs. K does."

"Remember when you told me you weren't going to let her tell you how to live?" she asked, pulling him around so he faced her.

"Yeah."

"So." She shrugged. "What's changed since then?"

He smiled at her reasoning. "Nothing." He stepped forward and, in front of everyone in the waiting room, he kissed her full on the mouth. She opened her mouth, and their tongues dueled. He pushed his hips against her, passion flaring up inside him. When clapping broke out, they jumped apart, looking around at the twenty-some smiling faces applauding their kiss.

Justin laughed. For a second, he'd forgotten where they were.

"Looks like the cat's out of the bag," Cass said. "Come on, we have a prescription to get." She pulled his on his hand, hauling him out to the car. As they drove to the pharmacy, she told him what the doctor had said.

He let out a breath in relief. "That's good news. And you have almost two weeks off, plus you've already run on the next track, so I'm not putting you back into the car until late qualifying Saturday."

"What will I do with all of that time?" she asked, grinning mischievously.

"You," he said, "are going to rest. If you want, we can fly back to Arizona and invite Brody and Jewel to rest with us. They seemed to be hooked together with glue."

He loved the way her eyes lit up when he mentioned taking her to his home. Hopefully, one day it would also be her home. He watched her close her eyes.

"That would be heaven."

Chapter Fifteen

Cass eased into the hot tub. Sighing, she dropped back her head. Justin watched her. She was so beautiful. Her long golden hair was piled on top of her head and some of the color had returned to her face in the last few days. She wore a skimpy bathing suit, revealing her curves under the water. Justin floated closer and slipped her into his arms.

"Hey, you two love birds."

Justin smiled at Jewel's call. Attached at the hip, Brody and Jewel sat across from him and Cass. Brody's arm was draped over Jewel's shoulder, and he smiled smugly.

"Don't you two have something else to do?" Justin asked.

As if he was waiting for a signal, Brody scooped Jewel into his arms and carried her out of the hot tub. "Yes, sir, I think we do," he said over his shoulder.

Justin heard Jewel's giggling trailing them down the hall. He leaned down and caressed Cass' neck with his mouth and tongue. Her satisfied moan vibrated in his mouth.

"Cass," he breathed against her neck, "marry me." His mouth trailed to hers to place a gentle kiss.

Her hands came up and touched his face. "You know I want that more than anything. I'm worried about the tour."

"We can wait until after the tour. I want you to finish. I can't say I'll ever be happy about what you do … but I know how important it is to you." He slid her body the last few millimeters to his, and his mouth claimed hers. He lifted his lips from hers. She made him wild with need, hot with desire. Before Cass, he'd never known such passion existed in real life.

"Yes." Her lips curved and she entwined her arms behind his neck.

He sighed in relief. *Finally, she's mine.*

She hugged his body against hers, her moistened skin rubbing against his. "Do you remember," she whispered into his ear, "the first time we made love here?"

He nodded as his hands moved under the water to ease off her bathing suit bottom. He had to have her. His heart ached for her love, and his dick ached for her body.

"Oh yeah, babe," he said, tugging off his own shorts, his erection pointing at her, "and the second and even the third." His hands moved to her ass. He positioned her on his erection, rubbing his penis against her clit. She moaned against his neck. He released her bikini top and covered her breasts with his hands, his fingers lightly pinching her hard nipples. He knew, as long as he lived, he would always crave her with the fire that burned inside him for no other woman, only Cass. He panted against her neck, hugging her. Caught up in the simple satisfaction of touching her, he climbed closer and closer to losing control.

"I love you, Justin."

He felt his heart swell in his chest and eased them both out of the water. He wrapped a towel around them, cocooning them together.

"And I love you." He rubbed her vigorously and smiled at her sensuous expression, her eyes at half-mast.

"I think it's time I got you back into bed."

He lifted into his arms, carrying her to the bedroom. He laid her on the bed and joined her, wrapping their entwined naked bodies with the comforter from the end of the bed. Their bodies sandwiched together, he stroked the wet strands of her hair off her face, running his hand over her shoulder to settle on her waist. His hand stopped its movements when he heard a feminine cry from downstairs. Cass eyes met with his, and they both laughed at Jewel's cry of ecstasy.

"Seems we created a house of debauchery here." He grinned.

Her laughter turned to a frown. "God, she's so young. I hope she knows what she's doing." She joined her hand with his and brought it to her mouth, kissing the sensitive part if his wrist.

His pulse accelerated. "She's nineteen years old, a woman. You can't protect her anymore. You have to let her live her life the way she wants. Besides…" He brought their entwined hands to his lips. Trailing his tongue over her pulse, he licked. She gave him that man-killing smile. "…If any woman knows what she wants, it's Jewel and…" He released their hands and wrapped his arms around her, absorbing her warmth. "…You. Let her be. You know Brody is responsible. He'd rather kill himself than hurt her."

Cass' hands curved over his ass. He was hard, hot and ready for her. He rolled over and brought Cass to his side, pulling her against his body. She caressed his penis. Groaning, he bucked against her hand.

"If you don't stop," he said, "we won't be getting any sleep."

Instead of replying, she slid her body on top of his, and ran her lips along his jaw. He sighed in pleasure, his hands running down her back to her hips.

"Did I say I wanted to sleep?" she asked.

Justin laughed, and laughed again when he heard Brody's masculine cry, deep, sensual and definitely satisfied. "I think I need some thicker w-w-walls," he said, stuttering when her kisses on his jaw turned to licks.

"I guess we better keep up with the Joneses." He ran his hands up to her breasts. "Can't have the kids outdoing us."

She leaned forward, her mouth on his neck. Then she licked down his body.

Justin released a long sigh. Soon his shouts of pleasure far exceeded Brody's.

~

The ringing phone woke them several hours later. He glanced at the clock: 3:00 p.m. On the first day of the start of their vacation, Justin had made Cass take a vow. For the next two weeks, they would sleep, eat, and make love anytime they wanted. Cass stirred against him as he reached for the phone.

"Hello," he answered sleepily.

Cass raised her head from his chest. He loved the way she curled against him in sleep. She gently rubbed a hand down the hard planes of his chest.

Then he recognized the voice on the phone. He sat up and Cass' roving hand stopped.

Cass saw the frown on Justin's face. "Yes, she's here," he said, his voice reluctant. She sat up and tried to push the disarrayed mop of her hair out of her eyes. She had the feeling she wasn't going to like this call any more than he did.

"Hold on." He reached over and punched a button on the phone, turning on the speaker. The voice that came over the line made her flop back down onto Justin's chest. He stroked her head.

"Cass, I'm calling to see how you're feeling." Mrs. K's stern voice said. She didn't sound concerned at all, more like *noblesse oblige.*

"I'm fine, Mrs. Kingsdale, feeling much better." Cass gave the expected answer, and Justin's hand clenched in her hair. She sat straighter and pulled his hands into hers. Massaging his hands, she tried to calm him.

"I also wanted to remind the both of you that the publicity surrounding your combined resting period hasn't left much to the imagination, as far as the press is concerned."

Justin's hand tightened on Cass'. Looking at his face, she saw something snap. His eyes met hers, as if asking for permission to speak. She nodded and ran her hand over his face.

"Listen, Mrs. Kingsdale," he said, "this is the way it's going to be." He stroked Cass' cheek, his eyes locking with hers, as if he was speaking directly to her. "Your laying down the law about our relationship is at an end. We're together and we're not hiding it anymore. Lee and I will run this team as we see fit to win this Series. If you want to pull your sponsorship, that's fine. I'm confident we can find another sponsor right now without any problem."

Leaning forward, he framed Cass' face with his hand. "Your threats of pulling your sponsorship have no more weight with me. Hell, you almost made me kill my driver, running her so far into the ground she has to take pills to keep her food down. I'm not playing your game anymore. Cass and I agreed, there is only one thing more important than this Series—Cass' health. I'll do what I think is best from now on. If you don't like it, then hit the road." He circled his hands around Cass back and rested his forehead against hers. "By the way, we're getting married after the tour is over."

Cass smiled and dropped a kiss on his cheek in congratulations and support.

There was silence from the other end of the phone. Cass stared at the machine.

"Well, Mr. Steed, I think I understand your position perfectly and we will abide by your rules," she said icily. "However, if Cass does not finish as one of the top five drivers, we will pull our sponsorship."

Cass flinched. Like Mrs. K, she realized anything lower than a top five finish wouldn't give her the publicity she needed to gain a sponsor.

"Fine," Justin said, no hint of uncertainty in his voice.

Wrapping her hand around his neck, Cass gave him gave him a kiss that began with gratitude for his belief in her, then sparked into more. She forgot where she was. Justin always made her passionate nature bubble to the surface. Mrs. K's squawk brought her back.

"Cass, I hope you're comfortable with who you've teamed with."

She laughed as Justin flipped her over, fitting himself on top of her.

"Mrs. Kingsdale," she said, arching her head toward the phone, "I assure you I'm very comfortable with the man I'm teamed with."

He playfully bit her shoulder. His arousal was hard and proud against her. She reached her hands out to encircle his cock. She silenced his groan with another kiss. Nothing could make her doubt their relationship, not even Mrs. K's warnings.

"Very comfortable," she said, pulling away.

"Hmph. I hope you're getting some rest. You have eighteen more races to go, and I want to see a good showing."

Cass began to run her hands up and down Justin's dick. He pulled up and reached for the button on the phone.

"Goodbye, Mrs. Kingsdale," he said with finality, and pushed the button, leaving them in blissful silence.

"Now where were we?" he said, his mouth making a direct path toward Cass' breasts.

~

Much later in the evening, they all sat in the living room, Cass and Justin sipping wine, Brody and Jewel coffee. They were reviewing and critiquing Cass' run from the tracks they'd be visiting in the next three weeks, before the final race in Atlanta. Justin jumped up and headed for the kitchen. "Anyone for popcorn?"

Everyone piped up yes. Jewel leisurely left the circle of Brody's arm to follow Justin, declaring she was going to help him.

Brody looked at her in surprise. Shaking his head, he asked, "How many people does it take to pop corn?"

Cass sipped her wine. Looking at Brody, she hesitated, and decided to take the plunge. "Brody, I know I shouldn't ask this and I suspect Jewel is doing much of the same with Justin, but I have to ask you what your intentions are with Jewel. She's young and she has goals."

His brow furrowed. "I've made no secret to Jewel about my feelings." He leaned back against the couch, shaking his head. "God knows she's a stubborn woman." He looked at Cass. "Kind of like another Jamison woman I know."

She arched an eyebrow. She wasn't going to let him get away that easily. She gave him a stern look that told him to keep talking.

"I know here," he said, placing his hand on his heart, "that she will always be the woman for me. It doesn't matter that we met a short time ago. I know I'll always love her. I asked her to marry me."

Cass leaned forward in surprise, her mouth open.

He held up his hand to stop her comment. "She said no. She wants to finish school. She wants more for us than this world we live in." He lowered his hand, running it over his face. "It's killing me that right now I can't make her mine for the rest of our lives."

Cass looked at him with sympathy. She felt a new respect for Justin's point of view, beginning to understand a little better why he had been pressuring her so hard to get married. She moved to the cushion on the loveseat next to Brody and hugged him.

"Don't worry. It will all work out. I know Jewel is stubborn. But I also know by the look in her eyes when she's with you that she loves you." She squeezed his shoulder.

Uncertainty lingered on his handsome face. In a little boy voice, he drawled, "Do you really think so?"

Cass laughed and squeezed him harder. "Yes, I think so."

They were smiling at each other when Justin and Jewel burst through the doorway, laughing. Jewel ran to Cass and flung her arms around her.

"I'm so happy for you."

Cass' eyes met Justin's, and he shrugged.

"Okay, tell me, what's this about?" she asked. Extracting herself from Jewel's embrace, she got up and plopped back down on the couch next to Justin, who was munching on the recently popped corn.

"That you and Justin are getting married," Jewel hugged Brody as she to fell onto the loveseat.

"Oooh, I see. Looks like my sister was doing a little grilling—while popping."

Justin grinned and plopped another piece of popcorn into his mouth, his other arm coming to rest on top of her shoulders.

"When?" Jewel asked.

Justin coughed and laughed at the same time, as if he was choking on the popcorn. Cass stared at him. Even with his face turning an unflattering shade of red, she knew in that moment she wanted to marry this man more than anything in the world.

He stopped laughing, the red fading from his face. As if he sensed her mood, his face firmed into serious lines. He set down the bowl of popcorn, his eyes hooded, waiting for her answer.

"Anytime, but we're kind of busy right now. We have eighteen races coming up with not much time to spare in between."

Justin gave her a satisfied smile and hugged her to him.

"Right after the last race?" he asked with question in his voice.

She nodded and was rewarded with a passionate kiss. They heard Jewel jumping up and down, squealing with excitement.

Cass broke away from Justin's embrace and laughed at her sister. The last time Cass had felt this carefree was before the accident that killed her parents. And she'd never felt this happy before she'd met Justin.

"Jewel, I would be honored if you would be my maid of honor."

Jewel started laughing. She bent down hugged Brody. He gave her a wide smile, his hands coming up to encircle her waist. She jumped on his lap and started listing off all the things she needed to do before the wedding, telling him it was only six weeks away.

Brody pushed her hair away from her face while she chatted. Love shone out of his eyes like a beacon as he stroked her jaw. Cass doubted he was even listening to anything Jewel was saying.

Justin pulled her off the couch. "Let's take a walk. It's a beautiful night."

Cass clasped her hand in his as he drew her outdoors into the cooling Arizona heat. He led her down a path behind the house, finally settling them on a ridge overlooking his surrounding property. It was a beautiful, sultry July night. Lights in the surrounding barn and stables winked up at them.

"How's the ranch doing financially since we started the tour?" she asked. "I know you were having a difficult time of it."

His arms came around her from the back and his head rested on top of hers. "Actually, the ranch has been flourishing this last year. With the money from the tour, I hired a foreman who has much more credibility in the industry than I do. He hired the people we needed to really make this a profitable business, made the connections I could never make. When my Dad died two years ago, he thought I had what it took to run this place. But as much as I was gone, racing most of my young life away, I didn't have a clue what it took to make this place successful." He paused, kissing her neck, sending shivers down her spine.

Cass rubbed closer, like a satisfied cat. No matter how long they were together, she knew his kisses would always arouse her.

"It's now a profitable enough business to proudly pass on to my children." he said against her neck.

In his arms, Cass tensed. It was the first time they had discussed having children.

"Cass," he said, turning her in his arms so they looked into each other's faces, "please tell me you want to have my babies?"

"Oh, Justin." She sighed and ran her hand along his jaw. "Of course I want to have your children. How could you doubt that?"

He blew out a breath and smiled. "Why do I feel a *but* coming here?"

"You know I'm not ready yet. I can't do what I do and be pregnant."

"Obviously," he confirmed. "When?"

"I don't know." She tensed, feeling his irritation. He had a habit of turning away when he was angry. She placed her hands on his shoulders and held him so he couldn't do it this time.

"Don't walk away. We will have children, you need to be a little flexible on this point." She felt his shoulder relax at her vehemence.

"You know, Cass, someday you'll be forced to make a choice between what you love to do and motherhood. I'm not getting any younger." He gently placed his lips on hers.

"I know," she whispered back, her arms running up his shoulders to caress the back of his neck.

"I love you," he said into her mouth, and deepened the kiss, his arms locking behind her back.

"I love you too." Cass angled her head to have closer access to his lips. "Old man," she added, and laughed when he growled.

His hands strayed to her bottom. Lifting her, he pressed her against his arousal. "Not too old to keep up with you, babe."

"You drive me crazy. I can't get enough of you. I don't think I ever will," she said, running her hands down his muscular chest to cup his balls.

His body automatically thrust against her hands.

She laughed at his reaction. "I'll take that as a compliment, I think." She undid his pants, her hands coming to rest on his penis. "For an old man," she murmured, "you're as horny as a teenager."

He groaned. She worked off the rest of their clothes, laying them on the ground to make a barrier against the earth. She pulled him to his knees and they sank down to the ground together. He ran his hands over her face down to her shoulders, then further down to rest on her breasts. He bent his head, his mouth replacing his hands, his tongue replacing his fingers.

"Do you think they will miss us in the house?" he whispered against her skin as she arched into his mouth.

"I don't care." She moaned, running her hands into his hair to massage his scalp. She heard him laugh.

It was quite a while before they returned to the house.

Chapter Sixteen

November
Atlanta Motor Speedway, Atlanta, Georgia
Final Race of the Series.

"I'll meet you at the track. I have to work on the car set up. We're going to switch the engine for the final race."

Cass raised her head from the pillow and waved, giving Justin a muttered response. As much as she loved him, she wanted him to go away so she could fall back asleep.

He kissed her on her forehead. "This is it, babe, the last race of the season. And not soon enough for me."

Without warning, she was hauled out of bed and into his arms. She screeched out her objection, wide awake now.

"Because tomorrow, you and I are getting married," he said against her neck, nuzzling her.

Laughing, she threw her arms around his neck. "Right, the best part of the tour." She kissed him on the jaw.

He gave her a quick kiss back, and laid her back into the bed.

"Got to go, see you at the track in…" he looked at his watch, "three hours." He grabbed his fuchsia Lovely Cosmetics jacket, scowling at it. "If I never see fuchsia again after this season, it won't be soon enough. Love you, babe." Not waiting for her response, he dashed out the door.

Cass yawned but decided she may as well stay up. She clicked on the TV. Watching NASCAR *Today*, she sat on the bed and weaved her hair into a braid.

"Okay, folks, three hours to go until the big race. The favorites today are, of course, Cass Jamison and Beau McCalister. They are within five points of each other, and today's race will determine who takes the coveted Nextel Cup. Let's talk about Cass Jamison, the Montana beauty, found by NASCAR crew chief Lee Gray and teamed over a year ago with NASCAR hero Justin Steed. This team has been an unbeatable combo, both on and off the track."

They flashed various pictures of the two of them at the track, signing autographs at the mall, clips of their Lovely Cosmetics commercial, winning in Darlington, then the final shot of Justin hugging her after her last race.

"Cass seems to have gotten back her health after a scare six weeks ago in Martinsville." They showed her smashed car. "After two weeks at Justin Steed's ranch in Arizona, Cass Jamison was ready to go, coming back to win at Charlotte Motor Speedway. Seems like more than racing stats was discussed during that rest period."

The picture switched to Justin and her at the airport. His arm was draped over her shoulders, both smiling they signed autographs.

"Rumors say that after today's race the two are heading for the altar."

Cass chuckled, amazed by the lack of privacy. Why did people care what she and Justin did off the track? All that should matter to the public was if they won or not.

"The biggest worry for Cass is Beau McCalister." There was a shot of her and Beau fighting in the infield of Daytona, then a succession of shots on different tracks showing their cars making constant contact.

"Sometimes you have to wonder if McCalister thinks this is a crash up derby, as opposed to stock car racing. Nevertheless, action will be tight at the Atlanta Motor Speedway, which is also the same speedway that ended the career of Justin Steed three years ago. Let's hope we don't see a repeat of that horrendous crash, folks, and good luck to Cass Jamison."

She grimaced at the reminder of Justin's accident. Nodding at the TV, she rose to get ready to head to the track. Just as she was putting on her fuchsia uniform, her cell phone rang. She answered it.

"Is this Cassandra Jamison?" a woman's voice asked.

"Yes," Cass answered cautiously.

"I'm so glad I finally found you, Ms. Jamison. I've been trying to track you down for several weeks."

"Who is this?"

"Sorry, this is Samantha with Semolia Medical Center. We were finally able to find your number. There was a little mix up with the file. I'm calling with your test results."

"What test results?" Cass asked in total confusion.

"From your appointment in October. I wanted to let you know your pregnancy test came back positive. I'm sure you already know by now. I wanted to make sure someone had reached you."

"What?" Cass froze. "Did you say I was pregnant?" Her heart squeezed in her chest.

This must be wrong. It couldn't be.

"That's correct. We wanted to make sure you contact your local physician as soon as possible to start your pre-natal care. I apologize for the delay. Please feel free to call us back if you have any questions. Here's the phone number."

The woman rattled off numbers that Cass didn't hear. Stunned speechless, she couldn't even say goodbye. After the woman hung up, Cass stood there, holding the receiver. Her hand moved down to her abdomen, as if she could confirm the news by osmosis. It all fell together now: the sickness, the tenderness of her breasts, her increased sexual appetite. Her hand moved from her stomach to her heart. She felt it pound beneath her palm.

Oh my God, I can't drive today.

Cass grabbed her gear and rushed out of the hotel.

I have to talk to Justin.

~

Everywhere Cass went, Justin had just left. Crew Chief meeting, checking on the car, setting the pit. Panic crawled up her throat; she was running in circles trying to find him. Her prep time for the race was getting slim and the pit crew was yelling at her to get ready. She finally found Darrin, cornering him at the pit.

"Where's Justin? I have to talk to him."

Darrin looked around, lifting his hand. "He was just here."

She saw what seemed like a sea of fuchsia jackets, but none were on the familiar tall frame. She cursed, and grabbed Darrin's arm. "Where's Brody?" she asked, desperation clamping onto her guts.

"He and Lee got caught up in an accident on the way from the hotel. I hope they're here soon."

The final call for drivers came. Cass froze. She felt frantic. Everyone was staring her, wondering why she wasn't getting into the car.

"Cass," Darrin said, "you need to get into the car."

She shifted her helmet in her hands and looked toward the car, biting her lip in frustration.

All the other drivers were out on the track and the NASCAR officials were calling for her.

"Tell Justin to call me as soon as Brody gets here," she yelled, running toward the car. She had qualified in second position behind Beau, and she needed to get set up or they would disqualify her. She decided she would hang back behind Beau and drive conservatively. At the first pit stop she'd have Brody replace her.

After she hopped into the car, she drew on her gear: her helmet and gloves, and hooked up her Com and fresh air. She eased into the line of cars, and moved the car back and forth to equalize the tire pressure.

Shit, I'm scared.

She jerked her hands against the wheel. Then she heard him.

"Sorry, Cass, I got caught in a Crew Chief meeting. I heard you were looking for me. Everything all right? You seem a bit jumpy out there."

"Justin, where is Brody?"

"Calm down. He's on his way, maybe thirty minutes out. What's the matter?"

She laughed in the Com when she thought about his question. She couldn't tell him over the Com. Everybody, including the press, could hear anything she said.

"Nothing, tell me the minute he gets here."

"No problem. How's the car doing?"

She frowned. She hadn't been concentrating on the car. Her thoughts were consumed with getting out of the race. If something happened to her, to her baby, she couldn't even think…

"Fine, it's fine." She went around three more times, trying to concentrate on her driving and keeping her line for the start.

"Watch the banking. It's twenty-four degrees on all sides, like in March," he said as she pulled in too tight on turn three.

"Okay, I remember." She panted into the microphone as she began sweating. The race hadn't started and she was falling apart.

"Cass, you're a half mile from the start. You've got to settle down a little."

"I know, I know," she said, hearing the panic in her voice.

Thirty seconds later, the green flag signaled the start of the race.

She managed to maintain her cool for thirty laps, none too easily. She had dropped to fifth place, trying to keep plenty of room between her and Beau, who was several cars front of her.

"Cass, what are you doing? Move up on Beau," Justin's voice squawked into the Com.

Cass gritted her teeth. "Where is Brody?" she asked as she made her way up several cars to position herself behind Beau.

"He's on his way right now," Justin said. "Cass, you're in second, look at taking him high on the third turn."

She shook her head. "It's too risky."

"What are you talking about? You did it in March. I have confidence in you. If you take the lead, you know he gets intimidated and you could lead the rest of the race."

"That was before."

"Before what?" he asked, clearly confused.

"Justin, it's too risky and I'm not doing it," she screamed into the microphone.

She heard nothing for a long moment.

"I'm not liking what I'm hearing," Justin said finally. She heard him pause to talk to someone next to him. "Cass, Brody's here."

She released a sign of relief as she fought to maintain her position. "Have Brody ready to go on the next caution. I'm coming in and he's replacing me."

She heard Justin giving an order for Brody to get ready to drive, then notifying NASCAR they were replacing their primary driver with the second. He didn't question her. He knew better. When she told him to do something while she was racing, he did it. The trust that had built over the year didn't fail her now.

"Brody is ready on the next pit stop, you need to move out quickly," he said. "Now … are you okay?"

Cass concentrated as a driver came up on her rear, attempting to take her position on the backstretch. She eased off on the accelerator, letting the other driver pass. As the car passed, it bumped her, causing her back end to break loose. She took her foot off the gas and lost two more positions.

I am worthless right now.

"Talk to me, Cass," he said, an edge in his voice she knew was worry for her and not the race. "You're losing position fast. Are you injured?"

"Justin, remember that conversation we had at the ranch, about me having to someday make a choice?" she asked, jockeying around for position, trying to avoid the other drivers.

"Yes." She heard the hesitation in his voice.

"Well, this morning I found out the choice has already been made for me."

She allowed him to absorb the news that had about floored her.

"Cass, you've got to get off the track. Now!"

"What do think I'm trying to do?"

"I'm not kidding, get off the track." His voice broke in her ear.

Suddenly, in her rear mirror she saw a commotion behind her.

"Please tell me somebody pulled a caution behind me," she pleaded.

"Cass, yellow out, get into the pits!"

"Get Brody ready."

Tucking behind Beau, she made her way to pit row. She started pulling off connections from her helmet and unstrapping various devices. Spotting her L mark, she roared into her position and, with Justin's help, bounded out of the car.

Brody was close behind her, jumping in. She helped him strap in as the crew serviced the car, adding gas, washing the windshield, and changing two of the tires.

She vaulted over the wall so they didn't exceed their amount of pit people on the track. Justin made sure Brody was set, then he snapped down the window net and yelled, "Go!"

Brody jammed out ahead of Beau. The exchange had taken all but thirty seconds, a longer than normal pit, but not bad at all. She knew she couldn't talk to Justin. Right now he needed to help Brody. He glanced toward her and nodded.

Cass gave him a thumbs up sign, then was swarmed by reporters, something she had expected.

"I'm okay, guys, not feeling my best."

They seemed in awe that she couldn't endure for the most important last race of the season. She gave them some spiel about the importance of safety and good health for the driver and how confident she was in Brody. Jewel, who had arrived for her wedding, appeared at her side and hugged her. Lee handed her a headset and she donned it, moving over to stand next to Justin. He gave Brody a position. When he finished, she gave Brody a rundown of the track conditions and how the car had been performing. He sounded pumped up to take the race and managed to maintain first position for over fifty laps before Beau started to dance with him.

"Stick with me, Brody," she said. "I'll tell you how to fight this asshole."

"Thanks, li'l lady, I appreciate that."

Cass stayed on the Com, giving Brody advice on how to handle Beau when he got too close or when she knew a move Beau would try to make. At one point, she felt Justin clasp her hand. She looked at him. He raised her hand up to his mouth and kissed her palm. With the love and happiness she saw in his expression, she made peace with her decision.

~

"Brody, you're putting on one hell of a race," Cass said, feeling pride well up inside her. Brody was a trouper. As a team, she was confident they couldn't be beat. Her eyes sharpened. "Brody, you have three laps to go off the caution. He'll try and come around to your left. Move left now."

Beau set up to pass and Brody blocked him.

"Keep varied movements back and forth to block him," she said. "Don't let him come up on either side. He'll try and take you out. Can you see how he's moving?"

Brody voice cracked over the microphone. "Yes, ma'am, I've got him." He continued to shift back and forth, successfully blocking Beau.

"Good, keep it up. Try to increase your speed. Bring it in," she said calmly.

Coming around the last turn, Beau tried to move to Brody's left, bumping his rear. He was trying to make him move, but Brody stayed fast.

"Good, keep your line. You're almost there, my friend," Cass said as Justin came up behind her.

Brody took the checkered flag. The crew erupted like a waiting volcano.

"Congratulations, Brody," she said into the Com.

"Couldn't have done it without you, ma'am." As he passed, he waved his gloved hand out the window, then promptly did a 360 on the grass, smoke rolling out of the back pipes. The sound of the crowd cheering was deafening.

"It's your glory now, take it. It looks like I'll be out for a while," she said, a small amount of sadness in her voice before she removed her headset.

Justin turned her in his arms. Although they were being jostled, people all around them, for her there was only the two of them.

He searched her face. She ran her hand over his scarred cheek, mouthing that she was happy to him. He mouthed back that he loved her. They couldn't hear any words because of the noise erupting around them. He hugged her, sandwiching her so tightly against his chest, she laughed. Picking her up, he swung her around. She knew everyone guessed he was just celebrating the win.

So they were. The most important win.

He set her down, then leaned forward and kissed her. In front of God, any reporters who cared to look, anyone else watching, he ravished her lips. Her arms went around his neck. The noise elevated as the crew clapped at their actions. Justin broke the kiss, pulling back. She laughed as he glanced around. Cameras and photographers surrounded them, capturing the kiss and the expression of love she saw on Justin's face and the one that must be on her own.

Cass stood in the circle of Justin's arms and met the onslaught of reporters. As soon as Brody drove up, the attention shifted. Cass and Justin stood back and let him bask in the attention.

"He deserves it," she said.

Justin nodded. Cass smiled when Brody kissed Jewel passionately, and enfolded her in his arms, ignoring the cameras and reporters. Then he moved over to Cass, dragging the attention with him. He grabbed her arm and raised their clasped hands together.

The crowd burst out screaming. Justin set his arm around her shoulder. Her heart raced.

Now, all my dreams have come true.

THE END

About the Author:

Rae Monet writes sensual historical paranormal romance novels and some contemporary for Liquid Silver Books and www.Triskelionpublishing.com. If you like strong female characters, lots of action, and hot romance, then you'll enjoy her books. Please take some time to surf her website www.RaeMonet.com and join her world.

Liquid Silver Books
http://lsbooks.com

Silver Net Community - meet our authors
http://lsbooks.net

More LSB Romances by Rae Monet

The Wolf Warrior Series
Rae Monet
    Solaria, a secret remote enclave in the Scottish Highlands, is home to the gifted Wolf Warriors. A home and a people whose existence is threatened by encroaching greedy English and Vikings, hunting the valuable wolf pelts. These are their stories of struggle, love and passion.
    The Lost Wolf Warrior
    The Solarian Raven
    A Viking's Vow

The Lost Wolf Warrior
Rae Monet

When Roan met the incredible Sable in extraordinary circumstances, he pieced together his purpose in life. But their journey is fraught with danger and a vengeful King. Suddenly they are protecting more than a society of gifted people; they are fighting for their lives, their love, and a fantastic legend.

The Solarian Raven
Rae Monet

Solarian healer Richard, on leave with Robert the Bruce, meets Megan, the one pure soul who can cleanse him. But an evil force is at work, and kidnapping Megan is the way to fire up an age-old clan feud.

A Viking's Vow
Rae Monet

At the close of the Viking era, Icelander Erik is hunting wolf pelts in the Highlands when he captures Sable, a Solarian warrior sworn to protect her animal kin. Which of them becomes enslaved, can they both be free to love?

Gabe's Prize (and Stolen Courage)
Rae Monet

SWAT leader Gabe has mastered all his demons. FBI agent Kally does everything by the book. On a bomber's trail, they shake each other's worlds as they discover that love won't be placed on hold in the name of justice.

Includes an extra FBI story, Stolen Courage.

The Best of LSB Romance...

The Zodiac Series
24 LSB Authors

12 books, a book a month from March 2005, each book featuring two stories about that month's Zodiac star sign.
http://zodiacromance.com

Ain't Your Mama's Bedtime Stories
Best Anthology of 2003 - The Romance Studio

R. A. Punzel Lets Down Her hair - Dee S. Knight
Beauty or the Bitch - Jasmine Haynes
Snow White and the Seven Dorks - Dakota Cassidy
Little Red, The Wolf, and The Hunter - Leigh Wyndfield
Once Upon a Princess - Rae Morgan
Petra and the Werewolf - Sydney Morgann
Peter's Touch - Vanessa Hart

Resolutions
4 ½ Stars Top Pick - Romantic Times BookClub

A Losing Proposition - Vanessa Hart
Free Fall - Jasmine Haynes
For Sale by Owner - Leigh Wyndfield
That Scottish Spring - Dee S. Knight

More Contemporary Romances from LSB...

Some Rough Edge Smoothin'
Louisa Trent
...sometimes sex is all a man and a woman really have in common, and sometimes that's more than enough... So it is with tough Latino Thomas and cynical Anglo Seraphina. Or is there more beneath the surface?

Love Lessons
Vanessa Hart
When solid friendship and passion collide, love is inevitable. This is the unexpected lesson for Wendy and Scott when she agrees to tutor him in the bedroom so he can try to win back his wayward wife.

Impatient Passion
Dee S. Knight
A few day off turning thirty-five and life sucks. Austin needs to make big changes. When an anonymous stranger pulls her close on the bus, she chooses to indulge. Austin isn't anonymous to Tyler though. He's waited long enough, now it's time to claim the woman he's yearned for.

Club Belle Tori
Michelle Hoppe
These two have it all, in spades. Jason Hunter has it all, in diamonds. Tori Lane has it all, in clubs. When their two best friends shuffle them together, can the millionaire and the pleasure palace owner have it all together, in hearts? Book I of the Club Belle Tori trilogy deals romance, passion, sexuality ... and wild cards.

Evening Star
Rita Sable
When Lilly takes a one-night job posing as an escort at a millionaire's party, she finds out that Gabe is more than she can handle…and everything she wants in a man.

Arrested
Alyssa Brooks
Handcuffed, searched, imprisoned … not exactly how Kristen imagined she would meet the man of her dreams. Will Reid believe in her innocence in time to save her life? Will her hellcat fire burn him or ignite long-dead carnal desire?

Teaching Elena
Maggie Casper
The problems start when Elena mistakes her millionaire landlord for a prospective employee. An employee she was planning would help her lose her virginity. One taste and she can't turn back.

Single Station
Rebecca Williams
Rory McKenna is no farm boy. He's too pretty for one thing and his approach to seduction is out of this world. Rory takes Samantha places she never knew existed. How far can a farm girl go before it's too late to come back?

Undressing Mercy
Deanna Lee
Tricked into posing for Shamus, Mercy finds both her career and her body in his very capable hands. Soon Shamus realizes that his interest is far more personal than professional, and he's breaking his own rules and discovering that there is something very different about undressing Mercy

Liquid Silver Books

Quality Electronic and Trade Paperback Books

http://www.liquidsilverbooks.com

Formats available:

HTML
PDF
MobiPocket
Microsoft LIT
Rocket eBook RB